NO DOGS ON MARS

A STARSHIP STORY

KEN KRAWCHUK

No Dogs on Mars
A Starship Story

www.Facebook.com/aStarshipStory
www.aStarshipStory.com

ISBN 978-1-7361354-1-9

Version 1.5
February 3, 2021
10-point Times New Roman
26,931 words total
plus a 6,598 word appendix

Cover art:
Front: James Parsons, Marc Bozzacco
Back: NASA/JPL-Caltech, Sonia O'Boyle
Venus Rising font: Raymond Larabie

Published by:
Amendment Sixteen Limited
PO Box 260
Cheltenham, Penna., 19012
info@AmendmentSixteen.com

Editor:
Henry Whitney
ESL Editing Service

DISCLAIMER

This novel is not sanctioned by or authorized by SpaceX, Tesla, the Boring Company, Neuralink, Elon Musk, the Great State of Texas or its cities, Friends of Bill W., Toastmasters International, Star Trek, the Association, Fireball XL5, Troegs Independent Brewing, or any other organization or individual explicitly mentioned or implied herein, and it does not purport to portray any of their ventures, initiatives, or past, present, or future plans.

For my dear wife, Roberta,
and her endless patience with my ramblings.

Chapter I – Mars

The Starship pilot bounced happily along the launch pad walkway, the low Martian gravity adding an extra spring to his step, a bounce he deliberately exaggerated. There was only one thought dominating his mind as he headed for his ship: *Tomorrow we leave for Earth!* Hot on its heels came a closely related thought: "With its excellent beers!" he exclaimed aloud, the anechoic reverberations loud inside the helmet of his surface suit.

In the near distance ahead of him gleamed his Starship, the *SxS Lathan Devers*, standing ready for the upcoming trip downhill to Earth. Its shiny stainless steel hull reflected the bluish hues of the early Martian sunset that streaked against the fading red sky. He stepped onto the waiting cargo elevator, pressed the UP button, and leaned against the railing nonchalantly as the platform swiftly rose.

From his ever-rising perch high alongside the *Devers*, despite the fading light to his left he had a commanding view of Elon City and the stainless steel forest of hundreds of fellow Starships standing sentinel on three sides of it. To his right, the fourth side sported thousands upon thousands of canted solar panels stretching farther than the eye could see, dipping beyond the oddly close horizon. Scattered among them towered innumerable cryogenic tanks holding the liquid oxygen and liquid methane created from Martian air and water to fuel the Starships' metalox rocket engines. An even greater number of cryogenic tanks were not in sight; they were buried deep in the Martian soil.

Come morning, virtually all those ships would be long gone—the *Devers* along with them—heading back to Earth to collect yet another consignment of colonists and cargo. A similar-sized fleet stood on orbit around the Earth in the final stages of refueling before transporting the next tranche to Mars. Conjunctions of the two planets occurred only once every twenty-six months, hence the current flurry of activity on and around both planets to take advantage of their relative proximity. The upcoming conjunction would be the thirteenth since the first two cargo ships lifted off for Mars twenty-six years earlier; and in the intervening decades, the fleets continued to grow.

Despite the pilot's anticipation of the plethora of beverage choices available on Earth, his exuberance was tempered by the thought of how his arrival there would unavoidably subject him to its arcane justice system once again. Too much of his previous layover on Earth had been spent navigating their slowly turning wheels of justice while trying not to get ground in their gears.

That layover had not been a pleasant one. It had made little difference to the prosecution that the pilot was only tangentially related to the charges they had lodged against the Company; still, he had quickly become their focus and target. Their paychecks came from the state, and having no incentive to pursue a quick resolution, they had drawn out the proceedings for as long as they possibly could. They knew a victory could be achieved not only by a clear conviction, but also through a stubborn tenacity that would eventually wear down their victim. It was a long-established fact that only one or two percent of all cases ever went to trial; instead, an exhausted defendant would typically plead guilty to a lesser offense just to bring things to a more merciful end.

The pilot, however, was not a person easily intimidated. He had known from the start exactly what the case was all about. The issue they had raised had nothing to do with him; it was all about the Company's sovereignty. Earth had never approved of the Company's terms of service that denied Earth any jurisdiction whatsoever over its off-planet dealings. Refusing to be daunted, the home planet had repeatedly attempted to assert its authority, thus far unsuccessfully. With this latest gambit, the pilot had merely been a pawn that Earth's rook had tried to remove from the interplanetary chessboard, a removal that could have resulted in far-reaching legal consequences.

But backed by the seemingly endless resources of the Company, the pilot and his legal counsel had chosen to face the rook head on. Their strategy was to take a page out of the prosecution's playbook by meeting every one of Earth's depositions with two of their own, thereby increasing the prosecution's workload geometrically with each filing. Eventually it was the prosecution who had thrown in the towel. Not only had the multiple filings required an ever-increasing time commitment from the prosecution, they also muddied the legal waters horribly. Not seeing any possible end to things, let alone a favorable one, when a critical filing deadline arrived the prosecution had deliberately failed to respond, thus surrendering. They would choose another battle come another day.

Although that final loose end had been neatly tied off not long before the pilot last left Earth for Mars, still he harbored a certain amount of skepticism about whether the legal circus was actually over. When it came to Earth justice, one could never be too sure of anything.

If there was anything good that had come from the protracted court battle, it was his acquaintance with his legal counsel—or, more properly, his captain's acquaintance with her. In passing, the pilot had introduced the two, and they immediately took to each other as if they were old high school sweethearts. Unsurprisingly, the pilot had begun to harbor concerns that the captain might decide to trade his space boots for bedroom slippers, but thus far those fears proved to be unfounded. The fact that the two men stood here on Mars was a confirmation of the captain's continuing commitment to the Company. Still, the pilot could feel the winds of change stirring the Martian dust.

The elevator came to a halt alongside the cargo airlock located at the bottommost level of the habitable portion of the ship. He manipulated the controls to open the outer door of the airlock, stepped inside, closed the outer door, and after swapping the airlock's icy, poisonous Martian atmosphere for the ship's benign one, he opened the inner door and stepped inside.

The pilot smiled as he began removing the helmet of his surface suit. *Just a few last-minute details to take care of aboard, and the evening is ours! Assuming I can coax our mooning captain out of the ship...*

* * *

The captain gazed absently across the Martian landscape stretching outside the ship's huge paned window, watching the blue sunset and thinking of Earth.

Over eight hundred ships for Junc-13! the captain marveled silently. *Over four hundred heading up, over four hundred heading down. And my first flight during Junc-4 left Earth with only twenty-five!* He shook his head, realizing how quickly those nineteen years had passed. *And there've been over four thousand transits without a fatality, too!* His spacer's instincts automatically shied away from the thought that perhaps one might be overdue, but he immediately quashed the notion. *I'm starting to sound like my lady friend on Earth.* But misgivings remained.

Thinking of her set his thoughts on a well-oiled track. There was no question he was eager to see her again—but was she just as eager to see him? He had been introduced to her during his most-recent layover on Earth, and the two had quickly become quite close. As the day neared for his departure for Mars, she took no shame in dropping many not-so-subtle hints that he could be much happier remaining on Earth than risking his life roaming among the planets. Too many times the visions she painted struck a very loud, resonant chord deep within him, sometimes to the point where he began to reconsider his resolve to roam. But such temptations had been the bane of sailors for many millennia, and whether it was sea or space, it made no difference. The distance and the dangers still remained, and many a love was abandoned—and sometimes lost!— in the pursuit of both. *And probably here's another love abandoned and lost,* he admitted, recalling their tearful parting when he last left Earth. He sighed aloud at the thought.

"Daydreaming again?" a teasing voice called out behind him.

Startled, the captain spun around. It was his pilot, of course. The captain hadn't heard his crewmate's approach because of the constant low drone of the ship's ventilation system that masked small sounds. Adding to the silence was the sound-absorbing quality of the padded carpeting that covered every square inch of ceiling, wall, and floor space inside the ship. The twin acoustic impediments easily swallowed up the sounds of the pilot's arrival. Still, the captain being surprised by the pilot's entrance was itself surprising. No one else could be expected to be aboard the day before their upcoming flight sunward.

Fortunately that trip promised to be an easy one: the *Devers* would be pretty much deadheading it back to Earth, carrying nothing other than the two men, their personal effects, and one convicted asshole. Unlike the transits uphill, on the downhill trip there'd be no colonists needing handholding, no cargo to load and secure, no unloading in Earth's immense gravity. The ship was a hollow shell, and even the LOX and methane tanks would remain a tad short of full, their total capacity not being required for so light a flight. The day had not yet arrived where any appreciable downmass would need transporting, nor was that day on the imaginable horizon. Some believed it would never come.

The captain returned his attention to the stainless steel forest. "Just taking in the view before we all lift in the morning." The scene that lay before him continued to tug at his attention. *So many ships!* He still could not wrap his head around the sheer unreality of it all.

"Yep. Daydreaming," the pilot confirmed with a smile as he stepped up alongside the captain. "Last looks and all that—and our last look for at least the next three years. Assuming you'll be coming back, that is?"

"Of course I'm coming back," the captain snapped, a tinge of annoyance plain in his voice. "You don't think I'd stay on lousy old Earth, do you?" Again, his thoughts returned involuntarily to the lady friend he had left behind, and doubts surfaced. He shook his head ruefully to shake them off and rationalized his reasons aloud. "Stay on Earth? With all that gravity? All those germs? And all the people? No thank you, sir! Mars is *so* much better, and zero G better still. 'All I ask is a tall ship and a star to steer her by,' as they say far too often."

"What?" the pilot replied, still smiling. "Not 'Third planet to the right, and straight on 'til morning?'" When the captain did not react, he added quietly, "Sorry. Stupid question, actually. After three transits as your pilot, I should know better by now. You'll be back. And back again. It's in your blood. " *I hope!* he silently prayed.

The pilot turned his attention to the vista spread out before him. In stark contrast to the stainless steel forest, the city itself was not much to see, spread out as it was over a wide swath of Arcadia Planitia and tunneled hundreds of feet deep. Most of the settlement area was flat, its reddish soil randomly punctuated by scores of domes of varying sizes spread out over a circular area miles across. At its exact center, dwarfing the domes, stood two gleaming Starships: the original two cargo ships that had established the first permanent human beachhead on another planet, the *SxS Heart of Gold* and the *SxS Bistromath*. Although both were theoretically capable of taking flight once again, their value as historical artifacts precluded any re-flight. Also, many of the internal systems in both ships were still in operational use, most notably the launch control room in the *Heart of Gold* and the so-called Room of Informational Illusions occupying the entire glass-walled prow of the *Bistromath*.

"So what are your plans for your last night on Mars?" the pilot inquired. Without waiting for a reply, he continued, "Me, I'm heading over to the Aleworks. You been in their new rave room yet?" Again without waiting for a reply, he added, "Haven't seen it myself yet. Been too busy getting ready to head for home. I hear it's a real trip, though. Be nice to see it before we lift. Last chance for a few years."

The captain did not respond. *Home?* he asked himself pensively. After nineteen years of plying the spaceways, he wasn't too sure exactly where it was he could call home. Come morning, home would be seven months in weightless transit, then home would be a year and a half waiting around in some deep, disease-ridden gravity well while the planets crawled back into position for the next junc. Waiting on Mars wasn't so bad, considering its much-lower gravity, pristine cleanliness, and germ-free environment. But waiting on Earth? He snorted his disgust at the fate that awaited him at the end of Junc-13. But the disgust immediately dissolved when he considered with whom he might be spending that time.

Misreading the meaning behind the snort, the pilot complained, "What's wrong with the rave room? Might actually be some available women there for a change, too. Few enough here on Mars as it is!"

"And those few available ones are no beauty queens either," the captain added disparagingly.

"Irrelevant," the pilot snapped indignantly. "When you can count the number of available women on half a finger,"—he held up a bent digit to underscore his point—"there *are* no dogs on Mars!"

The captain could not argue with any of the pilot's points. Although the human population on Mars was closing in on a cool hundred thousand, the overwhelming majority of colonists were men, and virtually all the women were already paired before they left Earth. The few unpaired women understood their immense value and pressed the advantage assiduously. Some of them went so far as to leverage that advantage into a commercial endeavor, calling themselves "free agents," even though their fees were far from free.

Over twenty thousand colonists were booked for Junc-13, but the male/female ratio was unlikely to change appreciably upon their arrival. Granted, the birth genders of native-born children clung close to the expected fifty-fifty ratio, but precious few of them had yet reached puberty—and parents tended to act quite negatively whenever any of the older men started sniffing after their fourteen-year-old daughters. Although the Company held a very loose leash on the Martian populace, that sort of behavior still fell outside the accepted norms.

The captain threw the pilot a cool glance. "I'd be careful not to let any of the ladies hear you referring to them as 'dogs'," he warned.

The pilot took on a theatrically perplexed look. "Didn't I just *say* there were no dogs on Mars? Besides, all women are beautiful. Some more than others, but beautiful nonetheless."

"Nice try. You'd do better changing the subject."

"And talk about Earth women instead?" he joked.

Refusing to take the bait, the captain remained silent.

The pilot turned and nonchalantly faced out the window. "Speaking of which, there's no reason we couldn't head for Earth right now. I just finished checking off the last few checklist items, so everything's secured for launch and ready for liftoff. In fact, all we'd need are the tanks filled, the elevator stowed, and the asshole aboard. But none of that's scheduled to happen until an hour or so before we lift."

"And that schedule hasn't changed," the captain confirmed while gazing out the window, unconsciously mirroring the pilot's nonchalance. "The tower still has us in launch position three hundred thirty-three."

The pilot added, "Nice. We won't need to be strapped in for fueling until dawn. Then it's 'on our way home,' as Robert the Robot would put it. But until then, the evening is ours." Smiling, the pilot mischievously started drifting slowly sideways toward the nearest ladder leading down to the control room where their surface suits were stored. "And let's not waste a moment of it!"

The captain could only smile in return.

The two left the lounge, climbing down the rungs of a well-padded ladder recessed into the wall, passing through the common room, then down past the two levels of passenger cabins and their corresponding storage cabins to the bottom level of the ship. Similarly recessed ladders were scattered everywhere throughout the ship; and while they wouldn't be quite so necessary once the ship was in space, they were a required feature while it was grounded. Just as necessary were the motorized platforms that would use the ladders as a vertical track to assist with loading and unloading passengers and cargo whenever the ship sat deep inside a gravity well.

The men entered the control room and retrieved their surface suits from their respective suit lockers and quickly donned them. They exited through the control room's airlock and into the cargo airlock directly across the narrow corridor, scant feet away. As per regulations, the pilot took the lead. When both were inside the lock, he cycled the inner door shut and opened the outer door, letting in a blast of frosty Martian air that they could not feel inside their suits. They stepped out onto the waiting elevator platform and sealed the outer door. The pilot pushed the DOWN button, and the elevator swiftly carried them to the planet's surface.

Stepping off the elevator and onto the paved launch pad, the two men walked to the nearest access port, cycled both doors on the airlock in turn, and stepped inside a climate-controlled tunnel some fifteen feet wide and almost as high. The walls and ceiling of the tunnel were circular, obviously having been created by a drilling machine, but the floor had been paved flat with a native cement to provide a smooth, broad surface.

After dutifully racking their suits inside the airlock, they sealed its door, boarded the waiting electric cart—automatically summoned by the DOWN button—and pushed the only control on the conveyance: a GO button. The cart accelerated smartly and followed the gently sloping tunnel downward, heading deep below the surface. Minutes later, the cart halted at another airlock. A sign affixed over the doorway read, *Musk*. Disembarking, they entered and cycled the airlock while the cart took its leave. As the inner door opened, they were met with a cacophony of sounds, followed swiftly by a mélange of odors: food cooking, mechanical tangs, vegetation, and, of course, human bodies.

"Ah, the lovely smells of home!" the pilot exclaimed, only half joking.

They stepped out of the airlock into a mammoth circular dome hundreds of feet in diameter and dozens of feet high, its triple-paned filterglass ceiling admitting the fading blue rays of sunset. Around the ceiling's rim was a veritable jungle of various plantings, some of them hanging down to a height almost within reach, but trimmed neatly to reach no further. At the floor level, the dome's perimeter was punctuated periodically with numbered airlocks, such as the one from which the men had emerged, each leading to a different cluster of launch pads. Wide corridors also emanated from the dome at the four compass points, and alongside each one was a dark, low-ceilinged tunnel with a single doorbell-like button alongside. Over the mouth of each tunnel was a sign identifying the tunnel name, each the name of a fictional or actual planet. The center of the floor space was dominated by a broad elliptical bar constructed out of native rock that could easily seat a hundred. There were no humans standing behind the bar. Rather, its inner circle was populated with nothing but compact food and drink dispensers within easy reach of the seated patrons. Suspended over the central bar hung a large, colorful sign inscribed with large, friendly lettering reading, *WELCOME TO MARS!* A smaller sign hung beneath it, in smaller lettering of the same font: *NO ASSHOLES, PLEASE.* Numerous high-top tables and bar stools were scattered all about the central attraction. Hundreds of people, overwhelmingly male, mostly in company uniform, occupied the room, drinks in hand. The dome buzzed with the muted sounds of their collective conversations.

An electric cart popped out of one of the compass-point tunnels bearing three men. The cart was roofless, doorless, and windowless, and sported on its nose the image of a stylized *T*. The cart's footprint was five feet square, large enough to seat four people in two rows of captain's chairs, and not much else. It halted and obligingly loitered as the three disembarked, then disappeared into the low-ceilinged tunnel. As the three walked away, an elderly couple stepped up to the tunnel and pressed the button at its side. The cart immediately popped back out and politely paused while the pair boarded. The woman said a few unheard words, and the cart took off down one of the compass-point tunnels.

The captain and his pilot remained standing at the airlock door for another moment, taking in the scene. The general atmosphere in the dome was festive, yet melancholy; no surprise, as most of the revelers were leaving Mars the next day and could not be expected back for close to three years, if ever.

"I am definitely going to miss this place!" the pilot confided enthusiastically, then quickly added, "C'mon, let's get out of here," and headed straight for the cart tunnel. He pressed the adjacent button, and the two clambered aboard the proffered cart. "Cart! Rave Cave!" the pilot directed eagerly. "Please," he finished, confirming the destination.

"Compliance," the cart responded. It accelerated smoothly, gracefully threading its way through the maze of tables, chairs, and people, and aimed for one of the compass points marked by an overhead sign reading *Anacreon*. The tunnel was a spacious one, significantly larger than the one leading from the *Devers*. It was easily wide enough for a cart to simultaneously pass along each wall, plus a roomy, lined walkway up the center for pedestrians. Side tunnels intersected occasionally, left and right, and at one point they came to a large circular room some fifty feet across and the same height as the tunnel, a lush lawn filling its center. The cart entered the roundabout smoothly and travelled around its edge for more than half its circumference before choosing a new tunneled route, its portal adorned with the sign, *Ceti Alpha V,*

"How far is this place"? the captain asked.

"It's under the new Douglas Adams dome. Not much farther."

The captain faced his companion. "Isn't that the other side of Asimov?"

"Yep."

"And isn't the Asimov dome the other side of Frank Herbert?"

"Yep."

"And isn't—"

"They recently opened a direct tube," the pilot interrupted, anticipating the obvious line of questioning. "As I said, it's not much farther."

As he spoke those words, the cart veered gently to the right into a tunnel wide enough for only one cart, then accelerated briskly. The tunnel was featureless and dimly lit, with barely enough light to see what was ahead. Between the lack of visible reference points and the smooth ride, it was impossible to tell how fast the cart was traveling. If not for the slight breeze against their faces, it would have been difficult to discern that the cart was moving at all. And that breeze itself could not be trusted, since an artificially created tailwind helped add to the illusion of immobility.

Soon they felt the deceleration, and the cart's path merged into a larger tunnel. "All right!" the pilot exclaimed. "We're almost there!" Slapping the captain's upper arm with the back of his hand, he added, "It's a rave!"

"We shall see," the captain replied, rubbing his arm theatrically. The pilot had an annoying habit of whacking a listener's arm when he wanted to drive home a point; the captain had a habit of reacting in an equally exaggerated manner. It was obvious the two had spent much time together, to the point where many of their interchanges seemed scripted.

Presently, the cart slowed and soon came to a halt. A long line of carts ahead blocked further progress. "I was afraid of this," the pilot grumbled. "The Boss is probably in there. He should stay the hell home, the damned old fart." He stood up in the cart, peering ahead, then turned to the captain. "Let's walk. It can't be much farther. I can hear the music."

The two men disembarked, and the captain ordered, "Cart. Go away. Please." In response, the cart replied, "Compliance," swung around to point in the opposite direction, and headed off. The two men took to the central part of the tunnel and walked in the direction of the hubbub. Before long, the two pedestrians encountered the same difficulty as the cart: there was no room to proceed any farther. The rave was packed beyond capacity.

"So much for that idea," the pilot admitted. "It'll be time to lift off before we could get in. Let's head to one of the other domes."

They turned and began walking in the opposite direction. Presently, an empty cart came up from behind and passed them by.

"Cart! Stop! Please!" they called in unison.

"Compliance," the cart dutifully replied as it stopped and let them climb aboard.

"John Steakley?" the pilot asked.

"Sure, why not," the captain replied. "They're all pretty much the same. At least Steakley is close, and not as likely to be so crowded."

"Okay. Cart. Steakley dome. Please."

"Compliance."

The pilot turned to the captain. "I, for one, am *not* going to miss hearing that word."

"You know, you can turn it off now," the captain informed him. "It's a recent update. Just tell the cart, 'No compliance.' It'll recognize your voice and it won't say it again in response to your commands. You can turn it back on by telling the cart, 'Say compliance,' or you can have it say any other word for that matter. Just tell the cart, 'Say X, not compliance,' and that's that."

"Why didn't I know that?" the pilot wondered, shaking his head.

"I just told you why. Because it's a new feature." Turning away, he added dryly, "Maybe you missed hearing about it because of all your excitement over the new Adams tunnel?"

Ignoring him, the pilot sat silent for a moment, then spoke, "Cart. Say screw you, not compliance. Please."

"Screw you," the cart dutifully replied.

"I can see how this could be fun," the pilot smiled, then sighed. "And we leave in the morning?" He brooded a moment longer, then added, "Now if only they can get rid of the 'Please' to execute a command."

"Fat chance of *that*," the captain replied. "You might as well try getting rid of the ENTER key on your keyboard. Besides, it's a safety feature to prevent unintended commands."

"I guess..."

Soon they arrived at the Steakley dome. It was strikingly similar to the Musk dome in size, format, furnishings, flora, and filterglass, as if the two had been built from the same architectural plans—which they had. But while the dome was far less crowded than Adams had been, it was clear there were many refugees from the overpacked rave. The two men took two of the few remaining seats at the bar, facing one of the dispensers.

The captain spoke first. "Bar. Bloody Mary, spicy. Please." A picture of the drink appeared on its screen along with the text, "□0.33." The captain extended his hand and touched his Company ring to the screen, and the image vanished. "Huh. The price went down again," he noted in passing. "Just my luck we're leaving tomorrow." Seconds later, a small door on the face of the dispenser slid upwards, and a plastic glass sat inside filled to the brim with the thick, red liquid. The captain retrieved it, and the door slid shut. He took a cautious sip and nodded his approval. "And I'm going to miss these! Not many people on Earth know how to make a decent Bloody Mary. Whoever programmed the dispenser software to make these babies really knew what he was doing!"

The pilot took his turn at the dispenser. "Bar. IPA with Bravo, Chinook, Mount Hood, Nugget, Citra, and Cascade hops. Please."

In response, the screen remained blank except for the words, "Sorry, not available."

"As usual," the pilot groused. "And I, for one, am *not* going to miss *that!* At least Earth knows how to make decent beer." He sighed audibly. "BarIPAplease," he rattled off quickly, hoping to confuse the dispenser's meager intelligence. But a picture of a half liter of beer appeared on screen, presumably an India Pale Ale, along with the text, "□0.25." He touched his Company ring to the screen and the drink appeared behind the opened panel. He lifted it out, held it up for a critical inspection, took a cautious sip, winced with a sour face, and added, "Too much Simcoe! Damned programmers." He took another sip and made another face, more theatrical than the last. "And exactly how soon do we blast for Earth?" he asked eagerly and just as theatrically. The captain did not trouble to reply.

As they sipped their drinks in silence, the pilot toyed with the ring on his finger. "The company has a real sweet deal with these rings," he observed. "They get to set the value of everything sold on the planet, control its distribution, essentially eliminate the black market, and all in return for the convenience of tap-and-go." He continued to examine the ring idly. "Maybe I should've had them size it for a different finger?" He proffered the preferred appendage.

The captain tried not to laugh though a mouthful of liquid. "Not while I'm drinking, please!"

"Seriously, how could we get around these ring things? Granted, someone could mine their own money, but why bother? Even Asshole City uses Company money. No matter what you want, at some point someone has to touch their ring to some sensor somewhere."

"Unless it's something the Company doesn't sell," the captain pointed out.

"On Mars? the pilot retorted. "What else is there to sell that the Company doesn't? Besides a decent IPA, that is," he added, pushing the half-full glass away.

"Tell that to the free agents," the captain mumbled, the comment passing unheard amid the background noise of the dome. Raising his voice, he added, "Just list it in your upmass manifest and bring your own hops. There's no law against it." *Or against free agents,* he noted in passing.

The pilot continued with his grousing. "Yeah? What about the cost of the upmass? Someone's got to pay the freight. And it's the Company that dictates *those* rates, too." He became more agitated as he spoke; something of a trademark for him. "And how many times has it happened that someone started importing something not on the Company's manifest? The first thing you know, it suddenly *is* on the manifest, and at a cheaper price, too. How can you compete against that sort of monopoly?"

The captain took another sip of his drink. "But why would you need to? If you and the Company are selling the same item, and the Company's is cheaper, why would I want yours?"

"Beats me. Dedication to free enterprise, maybe. Or family loyalty. Or just on general principles." He held up his beer at eye level, watching as the bubbles drifted up oh-so-slowly in the low Martian gravity. "Or pigheaded snobbery?"

"Wallow in it, then," the captain retorted, his tone of voice indicating he was done with the topic.

With matters of the Martian market behind them, their evening progressed more pleasantly. The two mingled among other patrons, most of them wearing the same company uniform as the captain and pilot. At one point, the captain was able to corral a pretty lady, the captain of the SxS Leto Atreides, who'd run every transit with her pilot husband since Junc-7. The captain cared not one whit for her looks, marital status or Company heritage; he was merely thrilled to be speaking with someone who was not male.

At one point, without preamble, their conversation was interrupted by a majestic low rumble that shook the ground beneath their feet. "There goes launch position number one, headed for orbit," she observed. "The Wyoming Knott, if I remember correctly."

"What position does the Atreides hold?"

"Three thirty-two." She held up her near-empty glass. "So I'm only good for the rest of this before I have to stop drinking. How about you?"

"Three thirty-three," the captain replied. "We'll be right behind you."

"True. And all the way downhill, too." She took another sip of her drink; something multicolored and unrecognizable that she called "an ultimate cooler."

"Your first transit down?" she small-talked.

"Nope. This'll be my fifth downhill. I recall my first, and how I was worried about how close the ships had sat when they were on orbit here. What made it worse is that since it's so highly elliptical, every few hours you're hurtling back to the planet at high speed before swinging back around. Add to that the fact that there's only a little more than a hundred miles between ships, once they're all up there. That's pretty close, as far as spaceships go. It was pretty unsettling at the time." He sipped his drink nonchalantly. "Not any more, though. You get used to it pretty quickly."

The woman smiled her agreement, adding, "One thing I find beautiful is that you can see the ships all lined up in a curved ring ahead and behind, shining in the sun like pearls on a necklace." Her eyebrows drew together. "But why worry? There's never been a problem yet; not even a close call. Starships have a perfect safety record."

Again, the captain's spacer instincts automatically steered away from the thought, but it left him uncomfortable in its wake. He masked his unease by draining the remainder of his drink. "You sound like my lady friend on Earth," he added wistfully, speaking into his empty glass.

"A lady friend?" she asked, not noticing the implications behind the tone of his reply. Before he could reply, she added with a dry chuckle and a wry smile, "In this business, it 's probably more likely to be an ex-wife."

The captain sighed at the possibility. "I suppose a lot can happen in three years."

With a start, she became aware of the emotional tenor behind the sigh. Realizing her faux pas, she suddenly became all concern. She touched him lightly on the arm and backtracked, "I'm *so* sorry! I should have noticed. You have 'future wife' written all over your face!"

He glanced up from his empty drink and just as quickly looked away. *Future wife?* He had never thought himself that easy to read. "Maybe," he finally admitted aloud, just as much to himself as to her. *Yeah, maybe... assuming she's not already lost to me!* Suddenly self-conscious, he stood abruptly, glass in hand. "If you'll excuse me, I should be calling it a night, seeing how we both have to get up so early."

The woman glossed over her own unease by taking the final sip of her own drink. "Good luck sleeping!" she warned playfully, injecting good humor into her voice to help lighten the mood. "Launch position number two is about to go off, and it won't stop there!"

"True," the captain agreed, mirroring her brighter tone. "Every few minutes there'll be another ersatz Mars quake."

She looked off into space dreamily. "You know, we're so lucky to be so late in the launch schedule. That means we'll be one of the last ships to leave orbit. I just love watching the ships glide out into space, one following the next. Almost like a waterfall—except it's not water and it's not falling." She giggled at her own weak witticism.

The captain basked in the sheer joy of hearing the clear laughter of a woman's voice. It immediately brought to mind the laughter of another woman, one who was many millions of miles sunward. Reluctantly yet eagerly, he turned to leave.

Maybe, he admitted to himself once again as he tossed his empty glass into the recycling chute. *Assuming she's still waiting, that is.*

Chapter II – Downhill

A dim blue dawn illuminated the captain and pilot in their surface suits as they leaned on the railing of the cargo elevator, the similarly clothed asshole at their side. The three rose swiftly up the side the *SxS Lathan Devers*.

Neither the captain nor the pilot could help but be mesmerized by the sight of the stainless steel forest that surrounded them, much thinned though that forest was. Over a hundred ships still stood around them, all in preparation to precede or follow the *Devers*. As they watched from the ascending elevator, in the distance another ship lifted itself from among its brethren on a pillar of flame.

Upon reaching the cargo airlock, the captain took one last look around while the pilot activated the controls to open the outer hatch. Once they stepped inside the airlock, the pilot retracted the elevator and sealed the outer hatch, swapped atmospheres, then opened the inner one. The trio removed their suit helmets and found themselves standing in the close quarters of a narrow corridor that circumscribed a central pillar. The pillar was almost a dozen feet in diameter and double that in height, formed out of a stack of circular sanitation facilities with the ship's control room at its base.

The captain turned to the asshole, speaking almost mechanically, as if in performance of a duty—which it was. "Pick any cabin on level two," he told the asshole, pointing upwards in the general direction of the ship's side hull. "That's where you'll sleep until we get to Earth. The dispenser's in the galley on the top level"—he shifted his pointing finger to the vertical position—"and the toilet facilities"—he shifted his pointing finger toward the oversized pillar that dominated the center of the ship—"are in the central core above the control room. Only use the top one, please; the three below it are locked anyway, and the bottom one is for me and my pilot. And be sure to read the instructions before you use it. There's no hotelier or domestics aboard, so please remember to clean up after yourself. Feel free to use the lounge, gym, and common room, but stay out of the other cabins. The electronics aboard all work the same way they do on Mars, so you shouldn't have any trouble adjusting. One of us will stop by before we land to brief you on procedures so you don't hurt yourself. Other than that, you'll be fending for yourself." The captain stopped and thought for a moment. "I assume you know how to remove the rest of your surface suit?"

"Duh," he replied scornfully. "I just put it on a few minutes ago, didn't I? I should be able to get it off."

"Do so now and stow it. We'll be lifting within the hour, so strap yourself in as soon as you get to your cabin. Any questions?"

"No, not at the moment."

"Good. And try your damnedest not to bother us."

The asshole glared darkly at the captain, but said nothing.

With that, the two men turned to go. Ignoring the obtrusive sign declaring *Authorized Personnel Only!*, with the captain in the lead they entered the open airlock of the control room. Behind them, the pilot secured the outer hatch and waited patiently inside the airlock while the captain doffed and stowed his suit before climbing into his chair. The pilot followed the captain into the ship's control room, securing the inner airlock hatch behind him. He removed and stowed his own suit and took the remaining chair.

Like the corridor and the airlock leading from it, the control room provided scant elbow room, and hardly anyplace to stand. The room was shaped as a hexahedron, barely eight feet across, five deep, and six high with two swiveling chairs equidistant from each other and the walls. The surface of all six walls was completely covered with high-resolution monitors to form one unbroken whole, although several of the monitors were mounted on hinged panels. One panel swung shut to cover the airlock hatch; another pair covered the twin closets holding their surface suits and emergency equipment; a third hid the door to the control room's rudimentary toilet facility. A narrow path, a mere six inches wide, stretched the few feet from between the airlock and toilet to between the chairs, threading its way between the monitors on the floor. Taken together, the monitors were able to provide a complete view outside the ship on all sides, minus the minor amount of space taken up by the footpath. Because the synthetic vision was so complete, no windows were necessary; and following the same reasoning, the control room was located deep inside the ship, just above the bottommost service level and closer to the ship's center of gravity to help reduce the potential for spin-related disorientation and its attendant artificial gravity.

The control room also hosted its own Environmental Control and Life Support System, independent of the ship's three larger redundant ones. The ECLSS maintained a livable atmosphere within the control room despite the airlocked seal that separated them from the rest of the ship.

Built into their chairs were numerous operational features, including a large gimballed screen that stretched from armrest to armrest and far over the knees of the chair's occupants, hinged on one side so that it could be folded out of the way as necessary. A flexible tube near the top of each chair provided drinking water on demand. It was from these specialized seats in the uniquely equipped room that the *Devers* could be controlled from startup to shutdown, from takeoff to touchdown, and every stage in between.

Both men pulled their control screens into comfortable positions above their laps, powered them up, and began the process of heading for Earth. Their first task was to establish contact with the control tower located high inside the *Heart of Gold*.

"*Lathan Devers* to Mars Control. Requesting clearance for launch," the pilot began.

"Mars Control to *Devers*. You are go for launch," came the reply.

"Roger," he confirmed. "Go for launch."

That simple task completed, they turned to activating the control room's monitors. Suddenly, the two men found themselves apparently floating in mid air high above the Martian colony, with the monitors presenting them with a complete view on all sides of the ship. The result was a very real illusion that the two observers were floating high above the ground among a forest of ships.

In stark contrast to the dramatic view that had opened up all around them, the final step before their departure was a prosaic one.

"Prepare for launch," the captain intoned.

"Preparing for launch," the pilot replied.

Each man pressed a specific virtual button on their lap screens.

"Launch preparations completed," the pilot reported.

"Launch preparations completed," the captain agreed.

With that, everything else proceeded automatically, with the process being monitored by the crew via their lap screens, by the launch controllers in the *Heart of Gold*, and by the ship's computers. Any of them could, at any moment, call a halt to the proceedings, but none was necessary. Under their mutual oversight, the valves were opened to begin the process of loading supercooled cryogenic liquid oxygen and liquid methane into the tanks aboard the *Devers* while innumerable diagnostic checks were performed on the ship and its systems.

During this time, the captain and pilot were kept very busy doing nothing beyond keeping a watchful eye as the launch procedures progressed. Both had been trained extensively and could, in a pinch, manually launch and land the ship; and indeed, a significant portion of the time the ship would be in transit would be spent honing those skills. But during this moment of truth, they felt more the passenger than the crew.

At the appointed moment, the *Devers* suddenly came to life. Flame blasted from its stern, and oh-so-slowly the ship lifted itself off the pad, the quick disconnects on the fuel feeds closing off any chance for backwash or overflow. Faster and faster the ship climbed into the reddening skies, and the view from inside the sphere of monitors was nothing short of spectacular. The ground dropped away, and soon the red sky ahead swiftly shaded to a deep black. Stars appeared.

The ship's comm system briefly burst into life. "Everything's looking norminal, *Devers*," the tower reported.

"Roger," the pilot agreed.

"Safe trip, *Devers*!"

"Thanks."

The captain huffed in annoyance. "I hate it when they say that."

The pilot threw him a perplexed glance. "Say what?"

"That 'safe trip' nonsense. It's not worth the effort of saying it, or making like they believe in any sort of superstitious luck. There's no such thing."

"What, you trying to jinx us, boy?" the pilot kidded.

The captain huffed once more and muttered something under his breath while pretending to study his lap screen.

Moments later, ahead they could see the sunlight glistening off the stainless steel hulls of some of the nearer ships already on orbit. Some were stationed equidistant from their neighbors, but irregular gaps appeared among some of the others. It was into one of the gaps that the *Devers* settled itself, its nose pointed only slightly above the ship in front of it.

"And that, gentlemen, is how we do that," joked the pilot, who had done nothing more than pushing that one button.

The captain, recognizing the quote, cast a dark glance at his pilot. "What, now it's *you* trying to jinx us, boy?"

"What, now it's *you* trying to ruin the mood, boy?" he mocked, whacking the captain's arm with the back of his hand. He waved the other hand at the monitors. "Look around! How many times have you seen anything remotely like *this?*"

"Lots of times!" the captain replied. "You knew—"

"Wait!" the pilot interrupted. Look!" he cried excitedly, pointing down at a moving speck. "Is that Deimos?"

"Doubt it," the captain replied calmly without a glance in the indicated direction. "The moon's thousands of miles below us, and, what, only five-ten miles across? Probably couldn't see it even if we knew where to look." He gestured at the monitors. "We wouldn't even be able to see the other ships if they weren't reflecting the sunlight."

The pilot was only half listening as he adjusted his lap screen to focus on the bogey below and tag it for identification. The image swiftly zoomed to focus on what was definitely another Starship heading for orbit. Under the image, the computers automatically added the text, *SxS Arthur Gleed*, followed by its velocity, mass, inclination, crew names, and a plethora of other parameters incidental to their curiosity.

"It's still boosting," the captain noted. "Otherwise we couldn't have seen it at this distance."

Their attention was snatched by another ship, this one much closer, nosing itself into orbit a few ships ahead of them. Idly, the pilot tagged it. *SxS Frank Poole*, it dutifully displayed, followed by a string of similarly needless information.

"Now," intoned the captain, theatrically settling into the deep padding of his chair, "we wait."

The pilot laughed out loud. "*That*, my friend, is the hallmark of space travel: the wait. Groundies always view space travel as exciting, but they never stop to think that the ups and downs last only a few minutes. The rest of the trip is a million times longer, all spent doing nothing but waiting."

As he listened, the captain began pressing virtual buttons on his lap screen, then looked to his crewmate. "It's closer to ten thousand times longer rather than a million," he corrected.

"Don't bother me with incidentals!"

"You'd better pay attention to such incidentals if you ever want to change your title from pilot to captain."

"Me? Captain?" he exclaimed incredulously. "No sir, not me! I'd hate to have the responsibility, not to mention the pain-in-the-butt factor. Don't make me remind you of that prima donna we had, what, three transits ago? *How* much of your time did she waste on that trip? It's bad enough our hotelier has to have his domestics cleaning up buckets and buckets of puke, flight after flight, but then there're always some passenger who feels they're entitled to special treatment, demanding to see the captain. Well, you can have it. No way I'd want to swap chairs with you." Dramatically, he settled himself firmly into his own chair.

He's got a point, thought the captain, but kept the capitulation to himself. Many a time he had wanted to just walk away from the responsibilities of command, be relieved of having the lives of a hundred people constantly in his hands non-stop, day after day after day for months on end. And then there was the constant lack of feminine companionship, a lack that tended to make itself felt more and more with time. His chat with the captain of the

Atreides the night before was the first appreciable time he'd spent with any woman in many a week. *But we're on our way to Earth,* he reminded himself, thinking of his lady friend who might be waiting there, not to mention the billions of other women who inhabited the planet if she weren't. But it wasn't the billions who drew his interest.

Of course he had stayed in touch with her during the years of his wanderings, but he still remained uncertain of her actual feelings for him, given that he had been absent for years. The root cause of that uncertainty was the unavoidable hurdle introduced by distance: no communication between the planets could be conducted in real time. The amount of time it took for a signal to reach from one planet from the other was never less than about five minutes, and typically ten to twenty minutes for most of the Martian year. That made normal conversation impossible. Adding to his isolation was the astronomical cost of communicating with Earth. Except for government-operated resources, the Company possessed a virtual monopoly on the communication links between the planets, and their pricing clearly reflected that power. If one believed all the Company's claims—about how limited the bandwidth was, about how much of it was used for official communication, telemetry, and commercial leases, about how little was left for lovelorn spacers—assuming all that to be true, the pricing might be accurate. But most doubted that. All that anyone knew was that text was dramatically cheaper than voice, which was incredibly cheaper than low-resolution video, which was an order of magnitude less than quality, full-color video. And during the weeks when the sun stood squarely between Earth and Mars blocking most of the usual signal paths, prices skyrocketed. The net result was that interplanetary communication for the masses was nearly universally text, with the same snail-like feel as playing chess by mail.

Still, at least he was able to stay in touch with her during his long voyage, even though the romantic content of most of their exchanges was along the lines of, "Hi. How are you doing?" But it would be months before they were close enough to Earth that he could hold an actual conversation with her. Until the day came when he could see her face and hear her voice, he could never be certain whether her feelings for him survived his absence; and that day was still a long way off.

With that thought, he suddenly felt the weight of the incredible distance that lay between them, literally millions of miles, and he unconsciously sighed aloud at the realization.

Upon hearing the sigh, the pilot ventured, "Sounds like maybe it's *you* who wants to swap chairs with *me?*"

The captain covered his unease with a devious smile. "Don't tempt me."

Hours passed as the final pearls inserted themselves into the orbital necklace. With its completion, the first ship fired its main engines in a trans-Earth injection maneuver and nosed out of Mars orbit, taking advantage of its position in the elliptical orbit to gain the maximum momentum advantage from being slung around the planet. Every few moments, as each successive ship attained its own ideal orbital location, its engines fired as well, unrolling the necklace of ships into a flaming silver chain heading for Earth. Starting with the lead ship and propagating to each follower, one by one, one after the other, the flames eventually extinguished, leaving each silver arrow in the hands of Isaac Newton and Walter Hohmann.

* * *

The days passed uneventfully as well as identically for the two men. So identical were their days that an outside observer would have great difficulty discerning which was the commander and which the first mate, because every twelve hours they swapped duties entirely. One man would always remain in the control room monitoring their progress and the health of their ship and its various systems, plus performing separate visual and audio inspections of the entire ship. The listening tours proved especially useful for exposing potential maintenance issues in their earliest stages.

In addition to that oversight, during their shift the men practiced an unending succession of simulations of various off-nominal situations, from something as minor as the loss of a steering jet to something as catastrophic as a full decompression of the ship. And should their electronic tutor find fault in its students' handling of the situation, it would replay the scenario again and again until they got it right. All the while, in the background the ship's computer kept a constant watch over their trajectory, occasionally making automatic adjustments to keep them on course. But there was never a need for the two men to interfere; the ship knew where it was going and kept to its course precisely.

A typical day for the captain would start with an exercise period to ward off the physical maladies caused by life in a zero-G environment. The medical and dietary supplements they ingested could only achieve so much, leaving exercise as a necessary component of any long-duration spaceflight. Next up in his day would come a large breakfast, after which he would relieve the pilot in the control room. There he would remain the full twelve hours. Near the midpoint of his shift, lunch was served in the control room by the off-duty pilot, lest the captain risk being absent at a potentially crucial moment while fetching lunch himself. After completing his twelve hour stint, he would be relieved by the pilot, and the next twelve hours became his own. The first item on the captain's agenda at that point was typically dinner, followed by all the mundane pastimes a person would partake of when nothing else pressed: reading, corresponding with those on Earth and Mars, and that one real boon to sanity: real-time conversation with the crews of the other ships to provide some much-appreciated human companionship. The net result was that the only time that captain and pilot ever saw each other were the brief periods when lunch was served and command was handed off.

In contrast to the orchestrated workload of the two crewmen, the asshole was left completely to his own devices, typically watching videos or playing games on his cabin monitor. But unavoidably, both men would encounter him from time to time around the ship. The captain pointedly ignored him with ill grace, but the pilot found in him a kindred spirit of sorts. When they first came across each other in the glass-paned lounge not many days after leaving Mars, the pilot's first words to the asshole were, "Dude! I hear that was a neat trick you played on the Company."

"Neat enough to get me exiled," he groused.

"Yeah, there's that," the pilot conceded.

"And I would've gotten away with it! Of all the lousy luck."

"How much did you skim off before they got to you?"

"Thousands! Well over ten thousand spaxars!"

"Whoa! How long did it take to land that much of a haul?"

"Over two years. Nobody notices the rounding errors when crediting accounts, especially when I limited the code to only divert anything beyond the fifth decimal place. No financial transactions ever go beyond the second digit, so the software they have in place never noticed such tiny discrepancies."

The pilot did some quick math in his head. "So you snagged, what, one fifty-thousandth of a spaxar on each transaction? On average, that is. Doesn't seem like much."

"Well, it becomes 'like much' when you realize that there are almost a hundred thousand people on the planet who average more than a dozen transactions a day!"

The pilot stared off into space, again doing the math. "What's that, fifty spaxars a day?"

"Closer to twenty, but yeah, you get the idea. I pulled in almost twenty K before they realized what was happening."

"How'd they catch you?"

"Luck," he spat out. "Pure, goddamned luck. *Bad* luck!" He stared angrily at the deck for a moment, then unloaded on the pilot. "They were preparing for a full-scale, system-wide simulation of the new transactional software release, when some jerk grabbed a snapshot of the entire live database for his testing. My software always cleaned up all traces of the diversion, *but...*" He paused and stared intensely at the pilot. "...that snapshot happened to sneak in *right in between the smallest of cracks!*" He held up one hand with his index finger and thumb a tiny fraction of an inch apart to drive home his point. "What were the *odds*, man? Billions to one? Trillions? That crack had to be less than a picosecond wide, but he got in! Then they used that snapshot to perform their full system-wide test, and one calculated total—*one total out of millions!*—came out wrong at the fifth decimal digit. Well, you know the Boss. If it's not perfect, it doesn't count. So they dug and dug, and it didn't take long for them to find my little electronic benefactor."

Though not a software engineer himself, the pilot understood how it happened. "Did they go through the formality of a trial? Or did you just fess up?"

"Fess up? Ha! That'll be the day! No, if they're going to rip my heart out, I'm not going to just hand them a spoon. They're going to have to come and get it themselves." He folded his arms to underscore that determination.

"Looks like they did," the pilot observed wryly. "But it looks like it's still beating, though."

"Ha-ha," the asshole mocked. "Very un-funny."

"How many were at your trial?"

"The usual. More'n five hundred, I'd guess, looking at how full the main amphitheatre was. Couldn't have been a thousand—that's all it holds."

"Sounds like yours was the only trial that day. Otherwise it'd've been packed full."

"Yeah—for all the good it would do me. It turned out the judge the randomizer picked was an old buddy of mine—for all the good *that* did me either."

"I don't see how it could've helped you in any case—pardon the pun! The judge is just a referee in these Martian trials, not like those power-mad, monopolistic, delusions-of-grandeur goth-like Earth judges in their black dresses."

The asshole smiled for the first time since coming aboard. "You sound like me," he gibed.

"Well," the pilot protested, "Who can pretend to like Earth justice? Or pretend that justice is being done there? When they stack the jury right in front of your eyes? When they lock you up for practicing law without their permission? Lock you up for questioning the judge? Lock you up just for breathing!" He became more agitated as he spoke. "Then force you to hire an overpriced specialist to navigate the convoluted, antiquated rituals that they defend tooth and nail? Tell me how it's any better a system than the divine right of kings! Well, it's not!" He stopped for a badly needed breath and gave a lopsided smile. "Yeah, I guess I'm a bit jaded."

The asshole laughed. "Sounds like you've had some first-hand experience with Earth justice."

"So how'd your trial go?" the pilot dodged.

"The way you'd expect. The randomizer picked thirteen people out of the crowd to serve as the jury, and no surprise two of them were software developers."

The pilot chuckled. "Only two? I'm thinking half the population of Mars must be nothing but software developers."

"Probably, but they weren't in the court audience that week. I guess they don't like performing their civic duty?" He waved the issue aside with a sweep of a hand. "Doesn't matter. Didn't take a whole lot of questioning from the jurors or testimony from the witnesses to get to the bottom of things. My only defense was getting them to prove it was me who did it, and not someone else using my user ID."

"I guess they proved it?"

"Yep. I pretty much expected them to be able to do that anyhow, because the final nail in my coffin was my own damned bank account—a lot more spaxars passed through it than I typically earn, and the difference closely matched the amount of missing money. So the next thing you know, the damned jury rules that I'm a Mars-certified asshole and not fit for the company of decent people. My sentence was immediate exile—*and* I had to pay back the money, most of which I no longer had."

"I imagine you accepted the sentence. You wouldn't be here otherwise."

The asshole snorted. "As if *that's* a choice. Either I accept the sentence and accept exile—the Boss has had a 'no assholes' policy at all his companies long before he left Earth—or I don't accept the sentence and live the life of an outlaw."

"Well, at least that *is* a choice."

"Not!" came the quick rejoinder. "If I don't accept the sentence, that means I don't accept the system of justice that sentenced me, and—"

The pilot was nodding, and finished the oft-repeated sentence for the asshole. "—and therefore can't call upon it to defend you if you're ever wronged."

The asshole turned away to stare a moment at the stars outside the broad expanse of the lounge window before continuing. "Well, I figured I'd take that chance."

"What?! You refused to accept the sentence?"

"Damned straight I refused. Like I said, I'm not going to just give in. *Screw* their 'self-governing principles established in good faith!'"

"Did you try to stay in your regular quarters or did you move into Asshole City?"

"Please!" the asshole implored with feigned diplomatic grace that bordered on being snooty. "We call it 'Uhuradelphia', or just Udel for short. It's a polyglot of Greek, Swahili, and Star Trek."

"Maybe you call it that. No one else does."

"'What's in a name?'" the asshole quoted. "It still stunk living there."

"How so?"

"Well, it was pretty lawless, as you would expect. If you live in Elon City, you know what they all say there: 'You have the right to live your life your own way without interference, provided you respect the rights and property of others.' Short and sweet, all twenty-two words of it. They have the kids recite it in school every day, like it was the goddamned Pledge of Allegiance or something. It's literally the only law they have on Mars. But not in Udel." The asshole shook his head and chuckled without humor. "Nobody there respects anyone's rights *or* property! Stuff would somehow vanish if it wasn't locked up or nailed down—and sometimes even if it were! Then there were the tough guys who'd put together their own little tunnel-states and play the grand pooh-bah to defend their turf. And more often than not they had these petty little squabbles—an outsider might call them 'wars,' except they weren't that dramatic—where ownership of certain tunnels would end up changing hands." He shook his head morosely. "I could write a big book about the shenanigans some of those guys pulled and how we peons managed to survive them."

"Sounds like these pooh-bahs were real assholes," the pilot kidded; but the subtle humor was lost on the asshole.

"Yeah, they were pretty bad. But it was tunnel space and food that were the biggest problems we faced."

"How could tunnel space be an issue?" the pilot wondered aloud. "The tunneling crews are everywhere, always tunneling."

"True," the asshole agreed. "But they work for the Company, not themselves. They tunnel where the Boss tells them to tunnel. But if you want your own tunnels cut,

you have to hire them through the Company's interface."
He held up a fist and brandished the Company ring he still
wore. "And tunnelers don't come cheap, believe me.
That's why Udel is mostly housed inside old mining tunnels
nobody wants anymore. It's pretty much only the poo-bahs
who can afford to cut new ones. And it's We the Peons
who end up paying for them with our extortion money—
excuse me, with our *taxes*." He spat the word out, then
added, "I am *so* glad the Boss left that barbarism to Earth
when he set up Mars. User fees make much more sense
than relying on theft at the point of a gun."

"Okay, I can understand the cost issue and the fighting
over tunnel space. It gets pretty tight everywhere whenever
the fleet arrives with a new batch of colonists, too. But
what's the problem with the food? It all comes from the
same recycled crap."

The asshole looks askance at the pilot. "Boy, you can
sure tell *you've* never visited Udel."

"Why's that? Food is food."

"True, but you're forgetting that software is software.
I can see you never tried to program one of those
dispensers. A good programmer can really make them
sing. Make a steak so real an expert couldn't tell it from a
cow. But a crappy programmer can't even hide the taste of
the crap that the food's made from."

"I certainly know about that!" the pilot agreed. "I
haven't had a decent IPA since I last left Earth."

"Yep, that's exactly what I mean. I'm an IPA fan
myself, and I can tell you categorically that no one in Elon
City has ever written a decent program that can make one.
Not sure why the Company hasn't bought any of the
commercial IPA software from Earth. They sure did
splurge on the dispenser software aboard these Starships."

"Agreed!" the pilot exclaimed. "What with all the
cash the colonists plunk down to get to Mars, it's the least
the Company can do to keep them well fed."

The asshole chuckled. "What was that old sci-fi
story? *To Serve Man* or something like that? The one
where the aliens used humans for food and no one knew
it?"

The pilot cringed. "Yuck! Never read it. Don't want
to even imagine it! Give me good old Starship food any
day!"

"Me too," the asshole concurred. "The food you guys got here is far better than anything they have on Mars!" He sat in silent reverie a moment, then added, "But in Udel it's not just bad beer; it's bad everything! All the dispenser software we have is either bootlegged or home grown, and neither one puts out gourmet cooking, if you know what I mean. But you do get used to it after a while, bilge though it may be. For over a year I put up with it."

"Yet you left?"

"Yeah, but not because of the food. Life in Udel started looking too much like life on Earth, what with the tin-plated dictators, the randomly changing laws, the graft, the taxes, the corruption..." He trailed off, staring out the window and into deep space. He turned to face the pilot. "So I figured I may as well opt for the real deal on Earth. At least the food would be better. So a few months ago I gave in and accepted the sentence of the court. That entitled me to a real chamber in a real tunnel in Elon City that's not hiding behind a crappy, under-engineered single-door airlock. But first I had to turn over all my savings toward restitution. *And* sign a promissory note for what I couldn't pay. Left me flat busted, it did. It's been three months since I gave up, but at least it's been a civilized three mo—" He stopped himself and scowled. "Yeah, right. How can you call it civilized when everyone treats me like a dog? Look at how your captain treated me when I first came aboard. 'Sit!' 'Stay!' Well, that's how it was in Elon City, too. A dog's life. Three months of it! At least I was able to land a relatively decent gig as a software tester to pick up some spending money while I waited for my ride to Earth to come along." He frowned sardonically. "At least the Company doesn't charge for the ride downhill. Small favor!"

"So what are your plans once you're on Earth?"

"Dunno. Probably have to get myself a real job to pay off that note. Ask me again a month after we get there—assuming the hellish gravity doesn't kill me first."

The pilot scoffed. "That's an old wives' tale. The tech today is really pretty good at stopping G-fatigue."

The asshole scoffed right back. "Assuming you can afford the treatments, you mean. My free ride downhill doesn't include those expensive drugs and stuff that you guys get gratis. All I get is the onboard gym."

"At least that's something."

"Sure it is," the asshole sneered. "Free stuff is always worth what you pay for it."

* * *

And so it went, the days stretching into weeks and into months, until one day that wonderful blue orb finally appeared as a fuzzy dot on the monitors, growing larger each day as the string of ships approached the Earth.

The first and only time the crew's carefully planned daily routine would vary was fast arriving: landing day. Then, regardless of who was doing what, both captain and pilot would simultaneously be on duty several hours before the final moment to prepare for and monitor the landing, and, if warranted, take command.

Their flight path and velocity had been carefully orchestrated throughout the entire transit to allow for a direct descent to the broad expanse of the Company spaceport in southeastern Texas. Although Earth-to-Earth Starship flights typically utilized offshore platforms connected to the mainland by 'loop or boat, the sheer size of the Martian fleet—and its non-stop growth year after year—demanded adequate elbow room. A fifty-mile square between Brownsville and Corpus Christi along the Gulf proved to be just the ticket—at least for the immediate future, because these days Starships were being constructed at the rate of four a week. Someday soon the spaceport would need to grow even larger to accommodate that constant influx, and no one was sure in which direction it would grow. The wildly inflated price of land in certain surrounding towns gave some indication, though; the Company was infamous for buying up entire cities at smugglers' prices.

On board the *Devers*, the pilot joined the captain in the control room, even though it was in the middle of his sleep period. But he showed no trace of tiredness or irritation. "This is it!" he gushed. "*Finally* I'll be getting some decent beer!"

And I'll be seeing my lady friend! the captain smiled. He had spoken to her—actually spoken to her!—and seen her image live!—just before going on duty that day, and she promised to meet him at the coastal spaceport. But best of all, the tone of her voice and the sparkle in her eyes told the captain that her interest had not waned in the years he'd been off gallivanting around the solar system. He was eagerly looking forward to that reunion, and it was obvious so was she.

Unlike the launch, there was no button that needed pressing; the two men had nothing to do other than keep an eye on things and be ready to take over as needed. The parameters for landing had been configured and entered into the ship's computers long before they'd left Mars. No surprise, the landing proceeded smoothly and according to plan. The *Devers* showed its belly to the thick Terran atmosphere and warmed to the task, its flipper-like fins expertly controlling its belly flop into the atmosphere. Sitting in the control room with the monitors giving a complete view of the fall, both men could be forgiven for their racing hearts, for the fall was as exhilarating as it was terrifying; because at seemingly the last moment, as the ship was apparently about to crash into the desert floor, the main engines roared into life, spinning the ship—and their stomachs!—as it pirouetted itself vertical. With a final gentle bump, motion stopped and the roar quickly died away. Small noises could be felt through the metal of the ship as it cooled under the hot desert sun.

The two men looked to each other and smiled. They were home.

Chapter III – Earth

The captain and pilot may have been home, but they could not move. The invisible hand of gravity held them firmly in its grasp, its power magnified by months of weightlessness preceded by more than a year of one-third G, and that preceded by another seven months of weightlessness. In an attempt to balance out that gravitational history, during the trip home they had gone through a regimen of exercises and drugs that would theoretically alleviate much of the impact of so immediate an immersion in Earth's gravity well. But despite that promise, simple motions became an arduous task. Their laptop screens became lead bricks. Standing became an impossible dream.

"You first," the pilot suggested.

The captain opened his mouth to respond, but thought better of it. Going first would be less effort than to continue squabbling, so he unlatched his safety harness, took one last sip of water from the tube alongside his face—even sipping was difficult in this dreadful gravity!—and with both hands on the chair's armrests, slowly forced himself to a standing position. A slight swoon accompanied his suddenly racing heart as it labored to keep the blood flowing to his brain. Presently he recovered and took the few shuffling steps to the airlock. Manipulating the controls, he opened both doors and staggered out into the lower cargo deck's cramped circular corridor.

A few moments later, the pilot stood at the captain's side, albeit unsteadily. The cargo cabins on the deck upon which they stood were typically full of the passengers' possessions during the uphill transit, but at the moment they were echoingly empty. But full or empty mattered little to the returned travelers; the most important feature was that the lower cargo level possessed its own dedicated airlock and elevator to the surface. Having that second airlock provided not only an easy way to load the passengers' cargo, it also provided redundancy in case the personnel airlock failed. Conveniently for the two men, the cargo airlock was located directly across the narrow corridor from the control room's airlock, limiting dramatically the distance they had to stagger.

The pilot opened the cargo airlock's inner door and tottered inside. No surface suit or other consideration was necessary, this being the home planet, so the pilot simply operated the control to open the outer door. There was a slight hiss as pressures equalized, and the two men found themselves basking in the hot Texas sunshine.

Squinting and grinning broadly, the captain turned his glittering eyes toward the pilot. "Home!" His thoughts were dominated by the imminent, intimate homecoming reception.

Weakly leaning on the airlock wall, the pilot asked, "Shouldn't we wait for the asshole?"

The captain looked him squarely in the eye. "Why's that?"

A half second passed. "Good point," he conceded. "Never mind."

As the pilot manipulated the controls to unstow the cargo elevator, the captain added, "He'll be by, by-and-by."

They stepped out onto the elevator's platform and sat down on two seats bolted to the platform's railing. The seats were mere metal panels, normally folded flat against the railing, but capable of being latched into a horizontal position to serve as seats. Although unpadded, the panels gave the new arrivals at least a place to take an incredibly heavy load off their feet.

The pilot pressed the DOWN button, and they quickly descended to the planet's surface. By the time they reached ground level, a familiar-looking cart awaited them, stylized T included, its dashboard sporting only a single GO button. They plopped heavily into its much-more-comfortable padded seats, and the pilot pressed the button. The cart trundled unevenly over the paved walkway now covered with gravel and dust kicked up by the landing, but it handled the challenge gracefully. Soon they came to a horizontal door lying on the desert surface. It lifted and hinged away from them, revealing a ramp into the desert underworld. Without pause, the cart rolled into the opening. The door swung shut behind them as they descended into cooler, conditioned air.

Several minutes later they came to a door which dutifully opened for them. As it did, a jarring clamor of sounds flooded over them—*much* louder than the Musk dome on Mars!—as the cart wheeled them into a massive, crowded terminal. Well over a thousand people and half as many carts and motorized wheelchairs filled the high-ceilinged building. Filtered sunlight streamed in through an expansive window-wall. Despite the bedlam, the cart knew exactly where it was headed, and when it arrived at a non-descript location in the middle of the terminal, it halted. Three people immediately descended on the cart: a doctor and his nurse—and the captain's lady friend.

"Welcome home!" she burbled through copious tears, awkwardly bending over the captain to bestow an unsatisfying, off-center hug. He blushed sheepishly at the attention, returned the hug as best his leaden arms would allow, and replied with a simple, "Hi."

While that homecoming celebration was in progress, the doctor and nurse helped the pilot into one of two motorized wheelchairs that stood at ready, then repeated the feat with the captain. Once they were seated, a large screen mounted on the back of each chair came to life, displaying the vital signs of the chair's occupants. The doctor studied the captain's briefly; the nurse, the pilot's. The two exchanged glances and nodded.

"Okay, everything looks good," the doctor proclaimed to the seated men. "Let's get you guys outta here."

He activated an unseen control on his wristband and started walking away. The wheelchairs automatically followed him, one behind the other, with the nurse and lady bringing up the rear. The troupe threaded its way through the throngs to the 'loop station, and there boarded a waiting pod sized to hold three times their number. The crew of another Starship was already aboard along with their medical entourage, and as the newcomers were fastening themselves in, a third group arrived. Warning chimes sounded, the doors silently slid shut, and the pod gently began to move. It quickly gathered speed, the acceleration similar to an aircraft on takeoff; a mere half a G. Once the pod hit its stride, the doctor and nurse unfastened their seat harnesses and fussed over the two men, administering drugs and taking measurements. For their part, the three passengers ignored their ministrations, instead chatting excitedly among themselves about Earth, Mars, the journey, and more. No topic survived very long, what with each of them interrupting the other with counter-stories, comebacks, segues, and more. Before long, the ignored medical team pronounced their charges healthy, and not much later the pod began its deceleration into Austin.

The Austin 'loop station was much less crowded than the spaceport's, giving the doctor a chance to brief the two men with fewer distractions. "Company policy says you can hold onto those chairs for four days," he told them. "But you should really get rid of them as quickly as you can."

"Four days?" the pilot cried. "What happened to the old four*teen* day policy?"

"There've been a lot of improvements in G-fatigue treatments since you guys left home," the doctor explained. "You'll be surprised how quickly you'll get your Earth legs back. The drug regimen you followed on the ship helps rebuild body mass much quicker, and the dosages are tightly coordinated with your exercise regime to get you back on your feet in a lot less time than before."

"How much less time? the pilot asked warily.

"The medication helps quite a lot, but it'll still be about a month before you'll be pretty much back to normal."

"About a *month?*" the pilot cried incredulously. "Wha'd'ya mean, 'about a month?' After being away from Earth for *years?* Last trip I was hobbling around a lot longer than that!" He folded his arms clumsily in the heavy gravity, looked away, and harrumphed. "I'll believe it when I see it."

"And you will," the doctor promised. "Another change to Company policy since you've been gone is with convalescent housing. We'll put you up at the facility for two weeks, but after that you're on your own. You can still use the facility for the exercising, but only on an outpatient basis."

The captain turned to the pilot. "There's your fourteen days," he observed dryly.

"Why didn't they tell us all this beforehand?" demanded the pilot.

The doctor chuckled without mirth. "That's Company policy, too. No reason to upset you with something you can do nothing about—and the Company doesn't want to have to listen to you whine about it all the way home," he added with a wry smile.

The humor was lost on the pilot. "So we've got two weeks to find a place to live? And most of that without the chairs?"

"That's it in a nutshell," the doctor replied. "You can extend your stay and keep your chairs longer, if you like, but at additional cost. Your rings will facilitate that."

With that, silence fell upon the troupe. The two men were not surprised at the changes, having just spent over a year on Mars putting up with the Company's whims. Apparently the whims were not quite behind them yet.

"I wouldn't be so quick to judge," the doctor advised. "As I said, treatments have come a long way since you guys left. You may not be dancing the polka when you move into your new haunts, but at least you'll be moving in under your own power. And the Company manages its own housing here in Austin, so finding a place to stay isn't an issue."

The captain's lady friend tightened her arm gently around his shoulder and smiled at him. "Don't you worry about that. You can stay at my place."

The captain met her eyes and held her gaze for a moment. Her eyes held the same sparkle he had seen from on board the ship the night before. His eyes misted as he replied, "Okay." There was no *maybe* about it.

"Hey, you guys got a spare room?" the pilot broke in.

The two looked at him a moment before the lady replied simply, "No," with a small smile.

"Thought not. Just kidding anyhow."

"And there's no need for you to stay with us anyhow," she added. "You and I won't be joined at the hip like we were the last time you were on Earth. Your court case is apparently still quite dead. I haven't heard a peep about it since you two were last here."

"No news is great news!" the pilot gushed.

"Maybe," the lady lawyer countered soberly. "They could always dredge it back up again, you know."

The pilot made a disparaging noise. "That's what I like about Martian trials—no appeals. And unless some witness lied or there's new evidence, a decision is a decision."

"As it should be," the lady agreed. Earth can learn quite a lot from Martian jurisprudence—except that I'd be out of business if they did!"

"Too true," the captain chimed in. "And you couldn't just turn around and hang out your shingle on Mars, either." He turned to the pilot and gave him a lopsided grin. "What was that you said about no dogs on Mars?"

"Hey!" the lady lawyer protested, feigning taking offense.

The pilot paid neither of them any mind. "Speaking of no dogs on Mars," he interrupted. "Or should I say, 'no hair of the dog'..." To everyone's surprise, the pilot suddenly spun his chair around, sped away at the chair's top speed, and called over his shoulder, "Pardon me a moment, but first things first." He crossed the broad tiled floor of the 'loop station and stopped in front of the first food dispenser. "Bar," he began. "IPA with Bravo, Chinook, Mount Hood, Nugget, Citra, and Cascade hops. Please." To his delight, the most beautiful image on the planet appeared on the machine's screen along with the text, "$105." He touched his ring to the screen and the text changed to "□0.03". He touched the ring to the screen again, and seconds later the dispenser's door opened to reveal its golden treasure. Reverently, the pilot gently lifted it out and took a sip, monetarily closing his eyes to savor the flavor. He slowly wheeled his chair around to face his companions, and despite the gravity he hoisted his glass high in both hands as if it were some sort of precious chalice; and in too-loud a voice, he proclaimed, *"WELCOME TO EARTH!"*

* * *

Readapting to life on Earth progressed even faster than the doctor had promised. Although polkas were not on the agenda within the first month, that milestone was attained not long after. The captain took up residence with his lady friend, as promised, and it appeared to be a long-term state of affairs. Right from the get-go he had his cache of belongings transferred from years of sitting in Company storage to her home, furthering evidence of a more-permanent habitation. All appearances were that he would remain there until Junc-14 arrived.

In contrast, the pilot chose to settle into Company housing for the long term. Starship crews were well paid, and his savings would cover the cost of the entire layover, and much more. Comparable non-Company housing in the area did cost a little less, but following that course would put him under the jurisdiction of Earth law rather than Company policy. He had had more than enough of that in the past, so rather than risk facing that particular evil again—maybe even face imprisonment without bail, should the dead case come back to life!—the only rational choice was the lesser of the two evils, evil though it may still be.

While captain and pilot fared well upon return, the same could hardly be said for the unfortunate asshole. When the ground crews boarded the *Devers* to begin the process of readying it for its next flight, they made a horrifying discovery: the asshole was dead. They found him lying on the padded floor of his cabin, its restraining straps unbuckled, with no sign as to what had felled the poor man. But a routine autopsy conducted later answered the question: the man had stood up too quickly, and his heart was not up to the sudden strain. Such a malady was far from uncommon; many a long-term Mars resident succumbed to a similar fate on returning to Earth. Those like the captain and pilot who received the proper medical prerequisites before and after landing usually fared well; those like the asshole, who had limited funds and could not afford the required regimen, often did not.

* * *

A few months after the return of the *Devers*, the Company circulated solicitations for Starship crews for the upcoming Junc-14, even though it was still well over a year in the future. Over five hundred ships would be heading to Mars that junc, one hundred of which would be enjoying their maiden flights. In contrast, over two dozen Starships would be making their sixth round trip, and the four oldest were on their seventh. To crew the vessels, in high demand were overly talented individuals who would fill the ship's seven billets: captain, pilot, doctor, hotelier, custodian, and two domestics. Only the best were recruited to fill those positions, and the competition for them was nothing short of fierce.

Within hours of the solicitation hitting the streets, the pilot invited himself to dinner with the captain and his lady friend to discuss the upcoming transit. He waited until dessert had been finished before he broached the reason for his impromptu visit. Nonchalantly, he asked the captain, "Think you can put up with serving me lunch for another seven months of twelve-hour stints?"

There was a short silence while the captain and his lady friend exchanged enigmatic glances, and without a word she began clearing dishes and left the room.

The captain took a deep breath and looked down at the empty spot where his dessert had been. "I believe I could," he began, speaking to the table. Uneasily looking up to the pilot, he continued. "I could," he repeated. "But the fact is, I'm not going back. Back to Mars."

Several seconds slipped by in silence.

"Not going back?" the pilot finally echoed uncertainly.

The captain took another deep breath. "That's right. I'm not going back." When the pilot did not reply, he picked up the narrative. "The lady and I have been discussing this since Junc-12. What she said made a lot of sense then, and she makes even more sense now. I never planned to do this gig forever, and what am I now, forty-something?" He laughed lightly at his own question. "It's easy to lose count when the length of your year keeps changing."

The pilot finally found his voice, and there was a barely detectible edge to it. "So that's it, then? You're just going to write yourself out of the next thrilling chapter of the colonization of Mars?"

"I guess you could put it that way," the captain conceded. "But you and I have written more than enough chapters to tee up the thrilling conclusion. It's past time for me to start writing a new story; an Earth-based story where our intrepid captain lives happily ever after."

Seconds passed in silence as the pilot slowly absorbed the new state of affairs, his shoulders slumping ever so slightly in acceptance. "So what drove the decision?" he finally asked. With a questioning glance, his eyes flicked momentarily toward the kitchen.

The captain looked toward the kitchen as well; it was obvious where his thoughts lay. He turned back to the pilot. "Yes, she's more than reason enough for me to stay. But there's so much more to hold me here."

"Like what?"

"Well, there's always been the danger factor involved when you're cooped up inside an air-filled bottle surrounded by hard vacuum for months on end."

"But the Starship's perfect safety record pretty much negates that argument."

"True, but like I said, there's so much more than that." The captain took on a longing look. "Believe it or not, I actually miss the Earth when we're away. I miss it so much sometimes it's almost a physical pain. Do you know what I did, right after the *Devers* landed and we came home?"

The pilot smiled wickedly.

"No, no," the captain quickly put in. "Well..., yes. But that's not what I meant."

"Should I ask? the pilot ventured, a faux-coy expression on his face.

"Doesn't matter. I'll tell you anyhow." His eyes took on an intense mien, as if he were revealing the truths of the universe. "What I did is that I took off my shoes and felt the good Earth under my feet. I loosened my Company ties and saw what it feels like to breathe. I took off my watch and found I had all the time in the world." He paused, his gaze still intense. "You want to know what I did? I found the secret to life: I took some time for living."

Seconds went by before the pilot replied offhandedly. "You're not fooling anyone. Those words are song lyrics. I couldn't tell you how many times I heard that tune in the background on one of my listening tours of the ship. You played it so many times on the transit downhill that even *I* could sing it. Can't say I know the band's name, though."

"The Association. Mid-twentieth century." The captain waved a hand, tossing the pilot's comments aside. "Doesn't matter who it was or who said it. The words are truer than anything I've heard in my entire life." He sat silent for a moment, then with an air of finality, he proclaimed, "It's time for living. I'm staying."

More seconds passed and the pilot tilted his head toward the kitchen. "Have you told her yet?"

The captain laughed. "It was she who told *me!*" A short moment passed, and he added, "She proposed. I accepted. Hell, I should've proposed to her before we left on June-13! But sweet dreams are made of these, and who am I to disagree?"

"More lyrics?" the pilot pointed out mischievously.

"More eavesdropping?" he inquired with a smile.

This time the silence between them dragged itself out. There was nothing more to be said. As if on cue, the lady emerged from the kitchen bearing a tray with three shot glasses and a bottle of bonded rye whiskey. "Anyone ready for an aperitif?

"An aperitif?" the captain asked. "Isn't it a little late for before-dinner drinks?"

"It's never too late for a drink!" the pilot interjected, whacking the captain on the arm. Absently, the captain rubbed the spot.

She reclaimed her seat, poured three shots and passed them around. "A toast! To our new lives!"

Looking to the pilot, the captain gestured with his glass. "May your departures equal your landfalls, and may all your landfalls be expected!"

The pilot looked from one to the other. "Guess I have to say something clever, too." He thought a moment and smiled. "And the best ships are friendships."

With that, they downed the golden liquid.

"I assume you're signing on again?" the captain asked his former pilot.

"Of course. It's in my blood. You know that."

"Going as a full-fledged captain this time? Not pilot? You have the required experience, as you well know. You have for several transits now. And the position pays a lot more. I'd be happy to vouch for you."

The pilot emphatically shook his head. "This is an old conversation we've had a million times. There's *no way* I'd want the responsibility of command. It's best to leave kingships to the kings."

"They'll probably assign you to a different ship, then. Not to the *Devers* again."

The pilot laughed. "So what? They're all pretty much the same. Like goldfish."

"There you go, trying to jinx yourself again," the captain warned. "Goldfish don't live that long."

"At least they have fun swimming around."

"While the fun lasts, that is," the lady added earnestly. "You can only tempt the fates so many times, you know."

The pilot scoffed. "'A ship in harbor is safe, but that is not what ships are built for,'" he quoted. "It's the fun that matters most." He held up his empty glass. "Speaking of which, does anyone else need a refill?"

Chapter IV – Uphill

Dawn found the pilot and his new skipper, a petite, no-nonsense woman with six transits to her credit, riding the passenger elevator up to the personnel airlock of the *SxS Red Shirt*, and a long ride it was—not merely because the personnel airlock was a few dozen feet higher than the cargo airlock, but more so because the *Red Shirt* was perched on top of another spaceship. Towering over the skipper stood the rest of the small crew that would figuratively hold the hands of ninety-three colonists for the next seven months: the hotelier, two domestics, the custodian, and the doctor.

The *Red Shirt* was poised and ready for its third transit to the fourth planet. It sat balanced on top of a virgin Superheavy booster, the *SxH Dark Star*, which would be boosting its first Starship to Mars. Like all Superheavies, it was named after a fictional spaceship. Neither ship nor booster were fueled yet, but all of the cargo, consumables, and passenger effects were already stowed neatly aboard. All that awaited completion was the addition of the crew, the passengers, and enough fuel to get them to their elliptical parking orbit. Once there, a series of tanker Starships would top off the *Red Shirt's* tanks as well as those of its five-hundred-plus fellow Starships. With that completed, the armada would blast out of orbit one by one and head uphill for Mars.

As the elevator continued its long ascent, the two domestics continued their verbal sparring with the hotelier.

"Nobody told me anything about anybody bringing any dogs," the senior domestic complained.

"Nobody told me either," his female apprentice countered.

The hotelier interceded. "Now, folks, it's just a rumor. If it were true, I certainly would have heard."

"Nobody's ever brought a dog to Mars before," the skipper pointed out.

"It'll have to happen eventually," the hotelier predicted. "Fortunately, not today."

The custodian chuckled. "Should be an interesting time when we do, though. I heard someone once took a lapdog on one of those point-to-point Earth shuttles, and the weightlessness scared the bejesus out of it. Whimpered the whole way, I hear. Made a real mess, too."

"And I ain't cleaning up after *scared* dogs," the apprentice insisted, shaking a finger at the custodian. "And scared or not, what's to stop the damned dog from pissing on everything everywhere? I can see it now: blobs of dog piss, floating all over the place—and worse things floating around too!" She turned to the hotelier. "We have those fancy toilets aboard for the people to use, but how you going to convince the *dog* to use one?"

"Why not just shoot the damned dog and call it a day?" the pilot suggested jokingly, tiring of the subject.

The apprentice grumped under her breath, "Sounds good to me."

The hotelier tried again to add finality to the conversation. "Let me repeat: No one is bringing any dog on board this or any Mars-bound Starship."

"That's what *I* say," the apprentice insisted irritably, intent on having the final word.

With that, silence descended upon the group. Only the muted whirring of the elevator could be heard as it lifted them higher and higher. But the stunning view more than made up for the lack of verbal stimulation. From their vantage point—now over twenty stories tall and still rising—they looked down on hundreds of Starships scattered across the Texan scrub. The *Red Shirt*, being the only ship in sight mated to a Superheavy, towered over them all. The apprentice domestic turned away from the vista to examine her feet, clutching the elevator's handrail all the tighter. Her acrophobia was showing again; an unusual affliction for a spacer.

"You all know what to do," the skipper reminded them. She swung her gaze slowly from one crewmember to the next as they looked down at her. "We've certainly drilled enough times this last year, but I'm required to tell it to you again.

"As soon as the pilot and I strap in, we'll be cuing Boca Control to open the passenger gates. They'll be coming up the elevator six at a time, maybe as many as a dozen, depending on whether they're two, three, or four to a cabin. You people"—he indicated the hotelier and two domestics—"will be at the personnel airlock to greet them and escort them to their cabins. When you get there, turn on the introductory video and make sure they're watching it before you leave. Figure you have ten-fifteen minutes between successive batches of arrivals, so you can take a few minutes to get the newcomers started."

Facing the hotelier, she added, "Most elevator loads will have a few priority guests. You'll be responsible for escorting them. I assume you know which ones they are."

The hotelier patted the device hooked to his belt. "Got all their names and pictures right here. I'm on it."

"Good." She turned to the doctor and custodian. "You two have all the luck. There's nothing major for you to do until either the ship breaks or a colonist falls ill. But at some point soon after liftoff, be sure to stop at each cabin and introduce yourself. We're going to be jammed pretty close together for the next seven months. Might as well get off on a friendly footing. Any questions?"

"Can we change the name of the ship"? the pilot asked jokingly. To his surprise, six angry pairs of eyes swung his way. "Huh!" he grunted, looking from one to the other in turn. "What did I say?"

The skipper drew herself up. "Our ship has a proud history, I'll have you know. And we're just as proud of its name!" She turned to the custodian. "Tell him."

The pilot folded his arms defensively. On several occasions he had heard others relate the story of how the ship had been named. It appeared he was about to hear it again.

"I guess the name was my fault," the custodian admitted sheepishly. "It was meant to be a throwaway name for a throwaway ship."

The skipper nodded her agreement. "They were testing a new flipper design and weren't sure it'd work."

The custodian laughed. "'Weren't sure?' We figured it would either work spectacularly or fail just as spectacularly! That's the problem with a forward-swept design. It could've given us a lot more agility, but the instability issues are pretty significant."

The custodian continued to expound upon his tale as if he were a professor addressing a class—a role he had filled prior to signing on as a member of a Starship flight crew. "Since we were so sure it was going to fail, we built this stripped-down Starship. Just a shell with no guts, not even a control room. Just the header tanks, engines, and avionics. We weren't even going to name it, it was such a throwaway. But at some point I happened to mention the parallels with the old Star Trek shows. It was always the nameless guy wearing the red shirt that got himself killed off real fast. Well, given the ship's redshirt nature, we started referring to it as the *Red Shirt*, and somehow the name stuck."

"Tempting the fates..." the pilot intoned ominously.

"Scotty was a Star Trek redshirt too, you know," the skipper quickly added. "And he was their *chief* engineer!"

The custodian nodded. "Yep. It turned out that Scotty must've been our patron saint because the test flight succeeded far beyond our hopes. So they subsequently outfitted the *Red Shirt* with all the interplanetary internal fittings and put it into commercial service. But we couldn't see fit to change the name. This'll be its fifth transit, and if there was going to be any superstitious trouble, we would've seen it on the first flight."

"True enough," the pilot agreed, attempting to bring an end to a second conversation he had tired of the moment it had begun. He regretted mentioning the ship's name at all. "It's a fine ship," he concluded.

The custodian opened his mouth to pick up the tale, but the apprentice domestic interrupted abruptly, momentarily braving her fear of heights by looking up from her feet. "Will there be any cats aboard?" she pointedly asked the hotelier. "Cats'd be worse'n dogs! Can you picture all those floating *hairballs?*"

The inscrutable look on her face left him wondering for a moment if she were serious or not; but a small, quirky smile quickly leaked out, giving away her game. They were still chuckling as the elevator halted at the airlock. The pilot operated the controls, and the assemblage stepped inside the *Red Shirt*. They were home for the duration.

The passenger boarding process took hours, but at least it went smoothly. At its conclusion, cryogenic fuels were loaded into the *Red Shirt* and the *Dark Star* both.

Finally, with the ships fueled, the last passenger aboard, the elevator stowed, and the airlock sealed, the control tower granted them preliminary clearance to launch. The lift-off siren blared loudly throughout the *Red Shirt*, and passengers scrambled to lie down on the padded cabin floors and secure the restraints that would keep them safe during launch. As each buckle clicked tight, the connection was electronically reported to a master display in the hotelier's cabin. As usual, it was necessary for him to chase down a few stragglers, but soon all was ready.

A duplicate of the master display was also available in the *Red Shirt*'s control room. Seeing the last red indictor turn green, the skipper intoned, "Okay, let's do this."

The pilot nodded and began manipulating controls on his lap screen. "*Red Shirt* to Boca Control," he began. "Requesting final clearance for launch."

"Boca Control to *Red Shirt*. You are go for launch," came the reply.

"Roger," the pilot responded. "We are go for launch."

"Prepare for launch, please," the skipper requested of the pilot.

"Preparing for launch," the pilot replied.

Each of them pressed a specific button on their lap screens.

"Launch preparations completed," the pilot reported.

"Launch preparations completed," the skipper agreed.

From there, the computers took control of the launch under the watchful eyes of the skipper, the pilot, and Boca Control. Tugging at the pilot's attention was the amazing view provided by the sphere of monitors that surrounded them. The passengers always found the huge glass-paned lounge to be the biggest attraction on board. *But that's because they've never seen THIS,* he told himself, admiring the godlike synthetic vision the monitors provided. More than once he had to remind himself to pay attention to the happenings on his lap screen, even though such attention had never been necessary. *Always a first time,* he reminded himself as he forced himself to focus on the lap screen.

At the appointed moment came the most amazing succession of sounds. The *Red Shirt* growled abruptly with a progression of lightning-quick spurts of turbulent shaking and thunderous explosions, each one louder than the last, until within a single split second the entire ship rumbled like a monster come alive. In the cabins, ninety-eight pairs of eyes were glued to their ceiling-mounted, in-cabin displays to watch the scene as the ship rose. Some chose to watch the wide-angle view broadcast from Boca Control; others preferred to look down from the stern cameras as the Earth dropped away; others favored the cameras in the prow, some facing upward, others downward. Those who had already mastered the controls on their cabin video screens were treated to all four views simultaneously on a split screen, or a succession of one perspective after the other, with the view changing every few seconds.

At first the massive ship hardly moved at all, apparently just sitting on the pad despite the hellish firestorm let loose at its stern. But lift it did, incredibly slowly at first, but picking up speed just as incredibly quickly. The artificial gravity from the ship's acceleration pinned everyone to their padded acceleration couch on the cabin floor with a force several times the gravity of Earth. For the passengers, it was the greatest thrill of their lives, an almost religious experience that brought tears to the eyes of most, misting their view of the large monitors affixed above them. The view ahead quickly darkened from deep blue, to purple, to black. A collective *Aaaaahhh!* filled each cabin as the stars instantly materialized, innumerable brightly colored pinpoints of light stark against the blackest black, with the squintingly bright swath of the Milky Way as their backdrop.

The reaction of the two crewmen down in the control room was identical to that of the passengers, despite the fact that both were veterans of numerous missions.

The comm system briefly burst into life. "Prepare for MECO and stage separation, *Red Shirt*."

"Roger," the pilot agreed. "MECO and stage sep."

With a suddenness that surprised every passenger, the rumbling growl abruptly ceased. A hundred stomachs momentarily bubbled up into a hundred throats. A massive *THUMP!* rocked the ship as the *Dark Star* disconnected from the *Red Shirt* and dropped away. Virtually no time passed when every rocket on the *Red Shirt* suddenly burst into loud life, pushing a hundred stomachs back to where they traditionally belonged. With only the distant stars as a reference, none could discern that the ship was travelling far faster than any aircraft in the history of humanity. And still it accelerated. Finally, after it seemed the growling would go on forever, again it abruptly ceased. Stomachs throughout the ship quickly returned to their non-traditional location as the artificial gravity dropped to zero; a state of affairs that would remain for the next seven months.

Strapped into their acceleration couches in their shared cabin, the two domestics turned to share a dour look. Soon they would be up to their ears in spacesick passengers—and share responsibility for the clean-up. Although the boarding process included fasting to help reduce quantity, the Groundies always managed to find something to expel.

Down in the control room, the skipper and pilot continued their vigilance. Veterans of many a transit, they were unaffected by the sudden loss of gravity.

The comm briefly burst into life. "Everything's looking norminal, *Red Shirt*," the tower reported.

"Roger," the pilot agreed. He waited as seconds passed in silence, then turned to the skipper and whacked her on the arm. "Did you hear that?"

"Hear what?"

"Nothing!"

Perplexed, the skipper had to ask. "Nothing?"

"Yes, nothing! He didn't wish us a safe flight!"

Turning away, the skipper merely rolled her eyes.

Moments later, ahead they could see the gleaming of ships already on orbit ahead of them. *How many times have I seen this view?* the pilot asked himself. *When will it ever become commonplace?* He automatically knew the answer: *Never!* Only a tiny fraction of all humanity had ever experienced the thrill of a Starship launching from Earth, and the pilot counted himself fortunate to be able to experience it not just once, but five times now. *And many more to come!*

The skipper turned to face the pilot. "It's time I head out to welcome all our passengers aboard, so you'll have the first watch. I'll be back in six hours to relieve you, and from there we'll take on the standard regime of twelve-hour shifts for each of us until we reach Mars." She unbuckled from her chair and floated toward the airlock. She faced the pilot one last time. "Looks like this is goodbye," she joked, knowing they'd see each other only briefly for the next seven months.

"Godspeed, skipper," the pilot called out to her departing back. "And have a safe flight!" he pointedly added.

* * *

Weeks passed as they hung there in Earth orbit waiting to be fueled for the upcoming transit, and not one of the passengers felt the least bit put out for the wait. Because outside the huge paned glass window of the main lounge, there before them floated the planet Earth with all its peoples, a glittering toy no one could resist; and no one ever tired of looking at the gigantic blue dot as it continuously rolled out from under them. The high eccentricity of their elliptical transfer orbit added to the thrill, sometimes bringing the Earth close to them, where other times it drifted farther away before drifting close once again. The pattern repeated itself every few hours, day after day, week after week as they waited.

Finally, the day came for the *Red Shirt* to be fueled. A series of tanker Starships would match orbits with them once every few hours, and the incredibly slow ballet that the two ships performed before docking was mesmerizing. One after the other, tankers arrived, transferred their load, and departed. And when finally the last one dropped off to return to Earth, the entire fleet was in readiness; the *Red Shirt* was the last of the lot to be fueled.

Moments later, the ship trailing them suddenly burst into brightness as its engines ignited for the trans-Mars injection burn. It swooped past them on its way to Mars, soon followed by the ship behind it, then the one behind that.

The pilot was on duty when the first of the fleet began its journey. Floating in the center of his visual universe, he watched as the ships blasted out of Earth orbit one after the other. Idly, he noted that the first ship to leave was the one immediately behind the *Red Shirt*, meaning they would be the last of the fleet to leave Earth, and subsequently the last to arrive at Mars; not that it mattered. What did matter is that the transit had begun. *Now, we wait... Seven months of nothing but waiting until we reach Mars.* The first exciting chapter of their journey uphill was over.

* * *

Life aboard the *Red Shirt* quickly fell into its normal routine. For the passengers, the experience strongly resembled that of the typical cruise ship that plied the oceans of Earth, except for one key difference: weightlessness. Just as some sea cruise passengers succumbed to sea sickness, most of the *Red Shirt*'s passengers were afflicted with space sickness. Predictably, most recovered after the first few days, but some of the worst cases lingered for weeks, challenging the high end of the Garn scale. During this time, the domestics earned their pay—and then some—as they chased floating globules of effluvia throughout the ship. But they took comfort in knowing that there were no dogs aboard. "Can you *imagine* that?" the apprentice fretted repeatedly.

One of the most important points raised in the introductory video that the passengers were required to watch was the operation of the personal sanitation facilities. Gone were all the abominations of the early space age: the catheters, the diapers, the notoriously unreliable vacuum-driven toilets, and worse. Taking their place aboard the *Red Shirt* was a simple solution adapted from an almost century-old science fiction novel. It was a near-circular disc some three feet tall and ranging between eight and nine feet in diameter. Whether the need was for shower or toilet, the process began the same: float inside, close the door, and push a button. At that point the entire disc would start to spin on its central axis, creating at its circumference an artificial gravity less than that of Earth's moon, but more than enough to ensure everything flowed in the proper direction. On one side of the "floor" of the cubicle, where its diameter was widest, there was a tightly lidded toilet bowl and standard-looking sink standing side by side, with a floor drain between them. One hundred eighty degrees away on the opposite floor was a meshed seat positioned over another drain. Affixed to the wall of the disc above the seat was a handy showerhead on a flexible hose. While the disc spun, artificial gravity would drive the grey water into either of the floor-mounted drains, the sink drain, or the toilet's outlet and into the ship's ECLSS so that the waste products could be recycled—a crucial necessity, lest the ship's water supply be exhausted long before their arrival on Mars. To lighten the stress on the ship's recycling equipment, showers were limited in both frequency and duration. As a result, shared showers had quickly become the norm many juncs ago, and were long advertised as part of the romance of interplanetary travel.

Outside the bathroom, the most difficult—and enjoyable—issue was adroitly maneuvering around the other portions of the ship in zero G. But many amenities were available to help alleviate the worst of the inconveniences. Velcro shoes were by far the most popular, especially since every flat surface in the ship was covered with padded carpeting. Velcro-seated pants made it easier to remain in a chair, especially at the lounge bar during happy hour. Waist belts, wrist belts, and ankle belts with dangling snap clip hooks instantly became the *de rigueur* fashion, allowing the passengers to easily clip themselves to innumerable rings mounted on walls throughout the ship to prevent them from floating away. The clips proved indispensible not only to keep a passenger in place while sleeping, but also as a backstop and fulcrum for amorous activities.

Unlike its seagoing cruise counterparts that sailed Earth's oceans and spanned time zones, standard time aboard the *Red Shirt* remained the same throughout the voyage, specifically, Texas time. Ambient lighting in the common areas of the ship matched it precisely, glowing brightly during the daylight hours, but dimming slowly as evening approached and going nearly dark come the night. Days of the week and dates in general aboard the ship also remained on Texas standard, the same as was observed everywhere off-planet. When living in any artificial environment, whether aboard a ship or confined to a tunnel on an alien planet where life took place out of direct view of the sun, naming the days and months became merely a matter of convenience. The Company could find no compelling reason for the ship, Luna, or Mars to deliberately place themselves out of whack with the mother planet, so they retained the ancient standards. In another nod to the needs of a passenger's circadian rhythm, upon landing both ship's clock and human biorhythms would be aligned precisely with that of Mars.

Despite the prominent dissimilarities between earthly cruise ships and Starships, there was one major similarity: a constant, steady stream of scheduled activities to keep the passengers entertained. The majority of these were indistinguishable from those offered by their watery counterparts on Earth. Some were pure spectator events, such as movies, recorded concerts, lectures on subjects of interest, even occasional presentations of legerdemain as performed by the ship's hotelier. Other events involved solid audience participation, such as talent shows, karaoke, trivia challenges, and the like. Of the unorganized activities, the most popular were card games. Out of necessity, these were played with magnetic cards on steel tables to keep the cards from floating away in the zero-G environment.

Some passengers took entertainment organization into their own hands. It didn't take long for a Toastmasters club to form aboard the *Red Shirt*, and their occasional speech contests were well attended by all. Inter-ship contests soon followed with Toastmasters clubs that formed on several other ships in the convoy, and before reaching Mars a Solar System Champion of Public Speaking was crowned. Other groups coalesced as well, such as the small clique who participated in daily meetings of the Friends of Bill W., and every Sunday morning Bible study was held in the main lounge while facing the glory of the heavens outside the ship's large-paned window.

As for activities for the lone individual, a passenger could enjoy any of the thousands of video games available though the ship's computer. For those who wanted relaxed company, facing the window in the main lounge was a convincing mockup of a British pub where the daily happy hour was held.

In addition to his skill as a thaumaturge, the hotelier also served as the ship's barber and hair stylist. A man of many talents, he had made it his personal goal that every passenger should enjoy every last minute of the long journey. In that, he had repeatedly succeeded. It was his dedication to service and his many talents that first qualified him for his position as hotelier, and they were instrumental in his retaining the position despite the flood of qualified potential replacements.

The same could be said for the doctor. In addition to the standard training any doctor receives, he was also a certified chiropractor, a board-certified psychologist, and a pediatrician, although there were no children aboard the ship this transit. Despite his diverse talents, there was little call for his assistance beyond the first few weeks of space sickness. The natural quarantine aboard the ship, and the month-long quarantine of the passengers and crew before departure, virtually guaranteed he'd encounter no virus- or bacteria-related ailments among his charges. As a result, his primary duty was to remind the passengers to utilize the gym equipment and to oversee their performance as they did.

Unsurprisingly, the custodian, too, was a jack-of-all-trades. Just as it was the doctor's responsibility to care for the passengers, it was the custodian's duty to care for the ship. In addition to earning degrees in engineering and theoretical physics, he had also spent his apprenticeship and early career in the Boca spaceport as a Starship assembler. During his stint there, he had devised several improvements to Starships, all of which had been incorporated into the *Red Shirt* and the rest of the Company's fleet. It was an oft-repeated compliment that he knew more about the innards of a Starship than the Boss himself. But the voyage proceeded smoothly, offering little opportunity for him to employ his manifest of manifest skills.

The months rolled past, one after the other, in blissful, weightless harmony. The worst the doctor had to deal with were the unavoidable bumps and bruises that Groundies often suffered before they developed their space legs. The worst the custodian had to deal with was an epidemic of cracked computer screens. The worst the domestics had to deal with was long put behind them with the welcome conclusion of the last case of space sickness, and the only drawback facing the rest of the crew and passengers was that hallmark of all space journeys: the months of boredom and waiting for it to be over.

* * *

The pilot came to.

His head groggy and sore, he lifted himself up from the floor. The first thing his addled mind comprehended was the presence of gravity. *Why am I lying on a floor?* he asked himself stupidly. Looking around, he next realized it was not the floor; he was lying on the flat surface of monitors which lined the inside walls of the control room. The monitors were active, but dark, leaking enough light that he could make out the dim outline of the twin chairs. One bank of monitors was skewed; it was the door to the sanitary facility hanging ajar. The monitors that he was lying upon were cracked and dark, most likely from his fall; more work for the custodian.

The pilot sat up, feeling the low strength of gravity countering his movements. After so many months in freefall, it took an overly conscious effort to coordinate his motions against the pull of gravity, feeble though it was. Slowly he brought himself to his feet, but promptly fell gently onto his side. *We're spinning!* he realized. Crawling to his chair, he gingerly pulled himself up into it and buckled its harness. He looked around at the dark monitors, gathering his thoughts. *I was coming out of the bathroom... There was a crazy-loud noise...* He pulled his lap screen into place and activated it. The familiar home screen lit up before him, brightening the close quarters of the control room. But where it typically showed row after row of green indicators for the ship's status, they were almost unanimously glowing red. *This can't be good,* he told himself, setting his jaw.

He activated the monitors that surrounded him, and their overly dim light did not brighten; but now they were covered with moving pinpoints of light. *Stars!* he realized. Their motion confirmed that the *Red Shirt* was indeed spinning end-over-end. Consulting the chronometer, he was surprised to learn he had been unconscious for almost four hours. *That must've been one helluva bump on the head!* he surmised. He pressed another virtual button, and a row of red indictors appeared with a single green one gleaming among them, revealing that atmospheric pressure had fallen to zero throughout the ship except for the control room.

Stunned, the pilot fell back in his chair, slack-jawed. *Dead? We're all dead in space? What the hell happened??* He activated the internal camera in the main lounge to begin a visual inspection of the inside of the ship, and he immediately had his answer. The upper portion of the paned window was missing, the adjoining panes bowed inward, and those not shattered were frosted over. Rotating the camera, he spotted the jagged two-foot-wide hole in the hull opposite the smashed window, dark stains on all sides. *A meteor! A meteor hit us!* He sat blankly as the realization settled in. *What were the ODDS? Billions to one? Trillions?* Returning to his video tour of the ship, he halted almost as soon as he had begun the moment he sighted the throng of bloated bodies pooled at the tip of the prow, held there by the spinning ship's pseudo-gravity. He slapped the lap screen to clear the morbid image, but it remained hovering in his mind. His hands began to shake, and he took a deep breath in an attempt to clear his brain.

Okay, enough of that! First things first... He activated the ship-to-ship communications system on the emergency channel. "Mayday, mayday, mayday!" he cried into the ether. "Starship *Red Shirt* declaring an emergency. Repeat: Mayday, mayday, mayday! Starship *Red Shirt* declaring an emergency. Mayday, mayday, mayday!" He paused, listening for a reply. Seconds passed. Half a minute passed before he repeated his call for help. Minutes passed, to no reply. He made a sour face. *Comm system must be down.* He sat thinking a moment, thinking, *Now what?* He had no immediate answer. *Wait! The convoy! Where's the convoy?* He manipulated the controls on the monitors surrounding him to focus on the fleet, but the ship's spin prevented any meaningful progress.

"Time to level this baby off," he said aloud. A quick scan of the propulsion systems using his lap screen provided mixed news. The main tanks and header tanks were intact, and the cluster of engines at its stern also seemed unaffected; but several of the bow steering jets were either disabled or missing. Had they remained intact, the *Red Shirt* would have long ago righted itself, but realizing itself damaged, the ship took no action.

Oddly, the pilot felt at ease with the situation. Many was the time he drilled emergency procedures for situations very similar to this. He swiftly and expertly configured the remaining steering jets to account for the missing; and after pausing to review his setup, he pressed the ENGAGE button. The spinning stars gradually slowed their sliding across the monitors, and the pilot could feel the gravity lessening. Moments later the stars came to a halt, as did the meager spin-induced gravity.

Returning again to his search for the rest of the ships in the convoy, he quickly located them. They were off to one side of his velocity vector by some five hundred miles and thirty-three degrees, and the distance between them was widening at over a hundred miles an hour. *That meteor sure packed one hell of a wallop!*

It was intuitively clear to him that the steering jets alone were not going to provide enough delta-v to bring him back on course. He'd have to fire the main engines to do that. Manipulating the lap screen, he computed the orbital mechanics necessary to rendezvous with the others. It would require a triple burst of thrust from the main engines to achieve his goal: one burst to adjust his current orbit to intersect with theirs, a second burn to position him back to his erstwhile position at the end of the line, then a third burn to match velocities. The pilot smiled. He could do that sort of maneuvering in his sleep! But when he configured the *Red Shirt* to perform the necessary maneuver, his smile quickly vanished; he found that the ship lacked sufficient fuel to effect the maneuver, let alone land afterwards. Had he been able to reach the convoy, he could have siphoned off a little fuel from each of the other Starships to give him enough to land. But since he couldn't get there, refueling was not an option. *And I don't have a working comm system to ask for the help anyway.* He immediately came up with an alternative: use the steering jets as a Morse code key. But just as quickly he jettisoned the idea. He'd need that fuel for the final approach to Mars. Stymied for the moment, he fell back in his chair to reassess his options.

Scotty! What do we have left? he joked. *Okay, I'm alive. That's a good start. The ship's alive too, and operational enough for the moment. Can't join the fleet. And due to the commutativity of orbital mechanics they can't join me either, even if I could raise them on the comm link. We're still months from Mars—assuming I can still get there?* He turned to his lap screen and quickly calculated the proper orbits and necessary burns to get him there; and again he smiled. *Yes! I still have enough fuel to make it to Mars and land!*

His smile quickly vanished. *At least at the moment, I do...* The longer he waited to correct his flight path, the less likely it became that salvation would remain in reach.

Coming to a quick decision, he announced aloud, "Okay, it's business time!"

Manipulating the controls on his lap screen, he configured the steering thrusters to orient the *Red Shirt* in the proper direction, and pressed the EXECUTE button. He felt the repeated puffings of the steering jets, and around him on the monitors he saw the stars reel. More puffings were felt, bringing the stars to a halt. Taking a moment to verify the ship's new attitude, he realized he could have effected the change with less fuel. Fortunately, the difference in fuel consumption was negligible, so his faux pas passed unpunished.

"Now for step two," he again announced aloud, as he configured the main engines for the proper thrust and duration. Once the task was complete, he paused momentarily to review his setup, more carefully this time in light of his previous oversight; because once initiated, the action would be irreversible, and his life hung in the balance. *Yeah, well,* he told himself nonchalantly as he pressed the EXECUTE button. Gravity returned again— several times Earth gravity—pinning him deep into his chair, with the growling that surrounded him reminiscent of the sounds of liftoff. For a brief time, the *Red Shirt* was a thing alive once again. Soon the engines shut down at the precise, prescribed moment, and silence descended on the ship as gravity once again vanished and weightlessness returned. He immediately began playing with the lap screen to confirm his new orbit, and he smiled. The plot revealed that he was aligned perfectly to reach Mars, and with more than enough fuel to land. Paradoxically, his new orbit would get him to Mars ahead of the remainder of the fleet. *Cool! I'll miss the rush!* he congratulated himself. *From last place to first place, just like that!* But his joyous mood was punctured when he recalled the scores of dead who'd be accompanying him. But there was nothing he could do for them now. His only mission was to save the ship, and this new orbit would do it. *And that, gentlemen, is how we do that,* he joked darkly.

With the immediate situation resolved, the pilot suddenly felt a strong urge to sleep. And why not? he asked himself. It's a natural reaction. And it's not likely there'd be another meteor passing through. I'm the only one aboard anyhow. He closed his eyes and immediately dozed off.

He awoke as quickly as he had fallen asleep; and according to the chronometer, he had slept for a little over an hour. Sipping some water from the tube alongside his head, he became aware of a need for solid food. With that realization, his thoughts froze. All the dispensers on board were outside the bubble of air and light inside the control room. They were all out there in the cold, hard vacuum of space. But he was not without the necessary tools to reach one. *No time like the present to start.*

Unbuckling his chair harness, he floated over to the locker where his surface suit was stowed. He swung open the monitor-clad door that covered it, extracted his suit, and conscientiously latched the door shut. He quickly donned the garment, a feat made trivial from long practice. But as he fitted the helmet, again his thoughts froze. *Oh, DAMN! It's a surface suit! Not a vacuum suit!* Granted, the atmospheric pressure of Mars was close to a vacuum—about a hundredth the pressure of Earth—but that last smidgen may prove problematic. Also, the protection the suit offered against cosmic rays was tailored for the surface of Mars, not for interplanetary space. Fortunately, the innermost walls of the passenger and cargo cabins were coated with radiation-blocking material, so at least the first part of his quest for food would find him behind their protective shielding. On the other hand, the dispensers were located near the ship's prow. There, the conventional Martian surface suit would offer only scant protection against a chance solar flare. But in light of his larger problems, that was the least of his worries

Only one way to find out if the damned suit is going to work, he concluded, and finished donning his helmet. After performing the routine system checks to ensure the suit's integrity, he propelled himself to the airlock, opened the hatch, stepped inside, and re-sealed it. He paused before activating the controls that would bleed off the air inside the airlock. He wasn't sure if the airlock had ever been tested against hard vacuum. But he immediately dismissed the thought, just as he had done with the questions about the suit. There was simply no other choice than to give it a try. Without food, he would surely not survive the months it would take to reach Mars. So without further hesitation, he operated the controls to evacuate the air. He heard pumps throbbing behind the wall and felt his suit slowly expanding due to the reduction in air pressure. He closely watched the airlock's pressure gauge as it dropped, his suited hands hovering over the controls, ready to take action in the event any issues developed. The drop in pressure slowed as it came closer and closer to a vacuum, and the suit began ballooning ever so slightly. Out of an abundance of caution, he pressed the button to pause the air's evacuation. The suit immediately ceased its expansion. When nothing happened for almost a minute he resumed cycling the airlock, bemoaning the fact that there was no control to moderate how quickly the air was removed.

Unfortunately, his caution proved founded. As the airlock neared the level of hard vacuum, the suit expanded a little further and a whistling hiss could be heard. Panicked, he halted the evacuation of the remaining air, but the hissing continued. "Damn it!" he yelled, his voice loud within the confines of the suit helmet, and he scrambled to reverse the airlock cycling. *Another couple of seconds and the damned thing might've popped!* If he ever made it home, he'd wager his life savings that the next Starship would lift with vacuum-rated suits.

Presently, with the return of airlock pressure, the hissing halted and the slightly ballooning suit resumed its normal fit. Once pressures had equalized, he opened the hatch to the control room and floated back inside. He paused while stowing the suit in its locker, wondering if the skipper's suit would exhibit the same weakness. But he quickly disposed of the thought of trying. She was a petite woman, and he was more than a foot taller; her suit would never fit him. Even her boots would be a tight fit if he wore them on his hands. Daunted, he latched shut the monitor-laden door and floated in front of it, thinking.

Scotty! What do we have left? he asked again, the joke quickly having worn thin. He looked around, and there were only four possible options: the suit locker, the airlock hatch—both of which did him no good—the sanitation facility—also equally useless—and the cubby holding emergency equipment.

Plan D, he thought to himself as he unlatched the monitors that covered the cubby. In it, he found numerous useful things, including many of the banal items that would be found in any emergency stash: an extensive first-aid kit, two oxygen masks each with a one-hour supply, a flashlight, and similar mundania. Some of its contents were pretty high-tech: a laser cutter, an emergency communicator, an air quality sampler, and more. Other items were decidedly low-tech: a crowbar, a hank of heavy-duty rope, and a hull patching kit to cover minor leaks—not very useful for the mammoth one that graced the prow of the *Red Shirt*.

"What, no offog?" he joked aloud once he had taken inventory. "What kind of ship is this?" His thoughts automatically turned to the late apprentice domestic, and his mirth suddenly sobered. She would have been thrilled to hear of the shortcoming.

Reaching around the impedimenta Velcroed to the cubby's walls, he pulled out the communicator, powered it up, and selected the Help function to find out its capabilities. As he suspected, it was a short-range jobbie intended only to contact adjacent ships or ground control, neither of which were within its range. He powered it down, reattached it to its niche, dutifully latched the cubby door shut, and floated back to his chair.

Now what? he asked himself. But he had no answer.

* * *

Weeks passed, but the situation had not changed, let alone improved. The stars still shone in the monitors, although the myriad pinpoints of light hadn't moved at all; not that he'd expect them to. Water continued to be readily available from the chair's feeder tube, and his ECLSS life support unit continued to keep the control room comfortable, although the ambient temperature had risen a few degrees. The pilot attributed the rise to an imbalance caused by the unimaginably cold environment in which the ECLSS unexpectedly labored. He counted himself fortunate that it labored at all. The sanitary facility also continued to function as designed, although it had been quite a while since there had been anything solid for it to process. Overall, the crippled *Red Shirt* behaved as well as could be expected as it inexorably followed the orbit the pilot had set it upon. Only once had he heard one of the steering jets puff briefly, but otherwise the ship proceeded as unerringly as a 'loop pod in its tube. There was no question the ship would definitely reach Mars, but by the time it did, all evidence was that it would arrive as a floating coffin.

Nevertheless, the pilot was never the type to give up easily. Not long after disaster befell the mission, he had researched the effects of a one-hundred-percent water diet, but found that no one had ever held on to the regimen for as long as it would take for him to reach Mars. Under the assumption that he might be the first to succeed—and not having any other choice—the next logical step would involve rehearsing the upcoming landing with a crippled ship. The ship's simulator was capable of configuring innumerable failure modes, including a breached hull, broken windows, and missing steering jets, thereby giving him the exact tool he needed.

His first attempt to simulate landing the *Red Shirt* on Mars failed miserably. The simulator revealed how hot gasses entered the breach while he was still high in the sky and quickly melted the prow, then even more quickly, the rest of the ship. Subsequent attempts using tweaks to the basic approach also failed completely, although the hull temperature did improve with each try. Eventually the stepwise improvements brought on by the tweaks leveled out, compelling him to devise a non-tweaky approach.

Going against all his training, he configured the *Red Shirt* to roll slightly to one side before entering the atmosphere, turning the hull hole toward the leeward side to protect it from the heat of re-entry at the risk of exposing some of the ship's windows. With the off-angle approach, it was subsequently necessary to alter the control laws of the four flippers which guided the *Red Shirt* through the atmosphere. Unfortunately he was forced to use a configuration they were not designed to withstand, so it was no surprise that his first attempt ripped the flippers clean off their moorings. Although by tweaking the tilt he was able to safely bring the ship lower into the atmosphere than all his prior attempts, every new attempt still ended in the same unwanted fireball. Still, it represented progress, and he patiently nursed the celestial headway he was making. Deeper and deeper his simulations took the tilted ship into the Martian atmosphere, canted, angled, and off-centered though it may have been. To protect the more-vulnerable windows from the heat of re-entry, he was forced to constantly alter the angle of the ship as it entered the atmosphere to allow them to cool. Any outside observer watching the landing would think the ship was tumbling toward a fiery demise.

But ultimately, he succeeded—almost—because after hundreds of attempts he was able to devise a solution that actually reached the Martian surface with the ship intact—but regrettably, the final flip maneuver ripped off its compromised prow, leaving the *Red Shirt* to crash in a ball of flame ever-so-close to home. Still, it was the best he had accomplished thus far, so he configured the computers to be ready to make the attempt upon reaching Mars.

Heartening though the solution was, improving upon it was becoming increasingly more difficult; not for technical reasons so much as for personal ones. As the days passed, he found himself becoming mentally more sluggish and progressively weaker physically from the lack of food. Often his thoughts would drift from the problem at hand, almost ceasing to function, until by sheer strength of will he brought his attention back to the issue of perfecting the simulated landing. Despite his handicapped state, he continued to make slow progress; but a workable solution to avoiding the final fireball continued to elude his diminished capabilities. At his current rate of decline, it appeared he would never solve the problem.

* * *

Over a month had passed, and in that time he had lost a substantial amount of weight and his mind had lost considerable functional ability, but he continued to plug away at possible solutions for surviving that final few hundred feet. The best potential option he had devised for avoiding becoming a part of the fireball himself was to literally abandon ship several hundred feet in the air, leaving the *Red Shirt* to its fireball fate while he plummeted to a messy death. The solution might have been made to work had there been a parachute aboard; but of course there wasn't. He considered trying to cobble one together out of his company uniform—he even had enough rope to string a makeshift chute together—but calculations proved it didn't have nearly enough surface area—nor Mars nearly enough atmosphere—to sufficiently slow his fall. And apart from that, simulations also showed how the uniform-turned-parachute would always burst into flames itself for the unforgivable and unavoidable sin of its proximity to the ship's fireball.

Not that he needed the uniform these days. The temperature within the control room had continued to slowly rise, but simulations fortunately predicted it would never reach dangerously high levels before the expected Martian fireball arrived. By then the internal temperature would reach that of a typical Texan afternoon. No surprise that as time progressed, his wardrobe dwindled to a pair of shorts.

In his hunger, one option he had considered was eating the unused clothing. Had it been made from cotton or wool, he surely would have tried. But it was constructed from some rip-stop synthetic that left it unchewable, and most likely indigestible. The gauze in the first aid kit also suffered from the same shortcoming. Time after time he took inventory of the few items available to him, looking for anything edible, but time after time he came up empty-stomached.

Eventually he reached the point where he was so weak physically and so befuddled mentally that he often stopped doing anything at all. For hours on end, he would just sit there in his chair snoozing and sipping water. He no longer pretended that the fireball was avoidable; and due to his badly weakened condition, even his last-chance swan dive now seemed impossible. And so he sat, not even counting off the days, waiting until the fireball came to greet him, assuming he survived that long. *If only there was something to eat!* he'd plead every now and again, in the increasingly rare moments when his brain decided to function; but it always ended with the same negative result.

The thought was again now in his head, followed quickly by the rejoinder, *but all there is here is—* With a jolt, he stopped the thought before completing it, as such a thought went against everything he believed. *But all there is here is—* he began again, rebelling at the idea before even considering it. *All there is...* he began again, again halting. *But all there is here is...* He steeled himself and forced his brain to complete the thought and finally managed to finish, ...*is me!*

He blinked several times to clear his eyes, forcing them to function as he looked downward, examining his bare feet. His thoughts slowly coalesced. *It...,* he began, pausing. *Could...,* he continued, pausing again. *WORK!* he finally finished with a flourish.

With great difficulty, he tried unstrapping himself from his chair. At first his ineffectual fingers refused to function properly, but eventually he succeeded. Drifting over to the emergency cubby, he made a clumsy attempt to open it. Once again his weak fingers refused to obey the dictates of his addled brain, yet once again he eventually succeeded. He hung there floating in front of the opened door for quite some time, marshalling his strength and occasionally forgetting his vital mission. In a moment of clarity and resolve, he reached inside and withdrew the laser cutter. He looked at it a moment, and on second thought, with his other hand he also extracted the first aid kit.

Returning to his chair while clinging to his prizes also proved extremely difficult. Time and time again he drifted past his chair and bumped into the monitor-covered wall before drifting away again. Ultimately he collided with the skipper's chair; but one chair would do as well as the other. Clumsily, he strapped himself in.

He powered up the laser cutter, its multiple deep red beams converging into a bright dot a foot in front of the device. He adjusted a knob, and the dot elongated into a sparkling two-inch straightedge. Hungrily, he stared for a long moment at his big toe; and steeling himself, he finally brought the laser cutter down. The motion was quick and decisive for a change, reflecting none of his mental or physical shortcomings. As it turned out, the first aid kit was unnecessary; cauterization did the trick more effectively than anything the ship's late doctor could have done. But he wished he had had the forethought of using the kit's local anesthetic.

No matter now, because dinner—a cooked dinner, no less!—hovered nearby, slowly tumbling end over end. As he reached for it, for the first time in weeks he began to consider the possibility that he might actually survive. If only he had the guts for it...

* * *

Almost a hundred thousand pairs of eyes were glued to screens large and small, in domes and private quarters throughout Mars, even in Asshole City, watching with frightened intensity as the crippled *Red Shirt* approached. It promised to be the first loss of a Starship after more than a quarter century of fault-free operation.

The thousands who understood orbital mechanics literally stopped breathing in fear as they realized the implications of the crazy angle with which the ship entered the thin Martian atmosphere. Ground controllers panicked as they computed the ship's trajectory to determine who was going to be engulfed in the impending fireball. Oddly, they noted how its impact point was located over the exact berth where the *Red Shirt* was scheduled to land. They breathed a sigh of relief when they remembered the fleet was still days away. Not only would there be nothing alive in the way, it would leave at least a little time to clear away the wreckage before the arrival of the remainder of the fleet.

To every single watcher, the fate of the *Red Shirt* seemed sealed when, at a point many miles high, it began tumbling haphazardly in all three dimensions. To the surprise of those in Mars Control, despite the gyrations, the ship still maintained a proper approach for the proper berth.

Scant seconds remained before the tumbling ship would meet its fate, when to the unanimous surprise of all, suddenly there were numerous, tightly spaced random plumes emitting from one steering jet after the other, twisting the tumble in unguessable directions. Incredulity was strained to the breaking point when without warning, the main engines ignited not fifty feet above the surface, each one gimballing wildly and spewing flames in seemingly indiscriminate directions. With that, the ship suddenly ceased its multidimensional rotations, and, like a feather falling on a pillow, gently set itself down in the proper berth in the proper orientation. With the banality of the ordinary, the engines shut down on contact. The *Red Shirt* was home.

It would be no exaggeration to say that at that moment there was absolutely no movement, no speaking, nor anything else happening anywhere on the planet Mars for several seemingly unending seconds. And the astonished jubilation that immediately followed was equally universal. Everyone on the planet over the age of sixteen had personally experienced the unavoidable fear that accompanied the belly flop flip when landing on the planet, instilling in them an equally universal empathy for others who also experienced it. Every one of them could easily see themselves riding in that plummeting, tumbling ship.

Ground crews waited impatiently inside the airlock to the surface while the berth cooled to tolerable levels. But they weren't the only ones waiting for that moment; for when they finally emerged onto the Martian surface, they could see the *Red Shirt*'s cargo lock already standing open, and a small, solitary figure in an ill-fitting surface suit riding down the elevator.

The elevator finally reached ground level, and its occupant appeared to be a child. He, perhaps she, hopped along the pathway using both arms in unison for locomotion, much like a monkey loping along through the jungle. The ground crew rushed to meet the new arrival.

Standing over him—and it was indeed a man, given the bushy beard behind the helmet's face shield—they saw he wore an unusually small pressure suit boot on each gloved hand. "I won't be needing these anymore," he declared as he tossed the boots aside. "No dogs on Mars!" He looked up as they towered over him, raising his arms to them as a child would, clenching and unclenching his gloved fingers. "Pick me up, will ya?" he commanded. "Walking around like this isn't as easy as it looks, especially after seven months of zero G!"

"What a landing!" one of the ground crew exclaimed. "We thought you were a goner! How'd you ever manage it?"

The pilot never paused. "Oh, I just had to chew over the possible solutions and find one I could really sink my teeth into. Once I got that first toehold, the rest was easy."

"Wow!" another exclaimed. "You'll have to tell me all about how you configured that landing."

"Careful what you ask for," the pilot replied. ""I might chew your ear off!"

"No, I'm serious. You should be teaching the whole fleet about that maneuver."

"Happy to help," the pilot replied with a smile, "I exist only to serve man... Kind."

As they fell over each other to lift him onto a cart, the pilot added with gusto, "Chauffeur!" He whacked the nearest man on the arm. "Musk dome, please, and on the double. And call ahead to tell them: 'Bar. IPA with Bravo, Chinook, Mount Hood, Nugget, Citra, and Cascade hops. Please.' And *don't* tell me it's not available!"

Epilogue

Relaxing in the Musk dome, the pilot sipped at his beer. It would be his last IPA before he headed downhill for Junc-15, and he was enjoying it immensely. But although it was made with the proper ingredients, there was something about the blend of synthetic Martian hops which lacked the depth of their earthly counterparts, sort of like a high-resolution image displayed on a lower-resolution device. *Well,* he rationalized, quoting from one of his favorite novels, *the astounding thing about a waltzing bear is not how gracefully it waltzes, but that it waltzes at all.*

He savored another leisurely sip. He was in no hurry to go; and they certainly couldn't leave without him anyhow. He let the beverage roll around his tongue, taking note of how artistically the flavor of the six types of hops harmonized. One of the best culinary programmers on the planet had coded it up for him as a "welcome home" congratulatory gift, even naming the concoction *Red Shirt Pilot* in honor of him and his ship. *F-H-I-P,* he paraphrased with a smile. *Fame Hath Its Privileges!*

On the dispenser's screen in front of him stood a live view of the former *SxS Red Shirt,* repaired, rebuilt and now renamed to be the *SxS Guy.* Come morning it would be blasting off for yet another transit to Earth, and he would be aboard. Only this time it wouldn't be as a mere pilot, but as its captain. His promotion had come hot on the heels of his arrival, once the details of his incredible journey had become known; and in his new role he had personally overseen the ship's reconstruction and enhancement.

Of the five-hundred-plus ships heading downhill, at his suggestion—and now standardized for all fleets—a ship similar to the *Guy* would be the last in line. Not only would it—and all other ships—have vacuum-capable suits and food dispensers in the control room, the *Guy* would henceforth remain uninhabited except for him, his pilot, and a specially trained custodian. Much of the space formerly used for passengers and their cargo had been repurposed to hold several additional cryogenic tanks to be loaded with fuel to serve as an emergency depot. Its hindmost position in the armada facilitated its potential use as a rescue boat for any future off-course Starship—not that anyone expected that to ever happen again. Still, one never knew.

The former pilot took another sip of his beer as he silently counted his blessings. *This gig is a pilot's dream! No crybaby passengers to worry about ever again! No overseeing of cargo loading and unloading in Earth's abominable gravity well! And best of all, a captain's pay for a pilot's responsibilities—not to mention a very generous disability kicker that was added to my retirement package after that last trip! In theory I may be the captain, but the reality is that I'm still just the pilot.*

Downing the rest of his beer, he walked from the bar to the proper numbered airlock door. With one final glance over his shoulder at the typical Martian dome scene, he cycled the airlock and stepped into the corridor beyond. There his cart obediently waited, but he decided he could do without it. *It's only three miles to the ship*, he told himself. *I'll walk it.*

He had long ago mastered the neural link that connected his thoughts to the mechanical legs he now wore. And since the bionics possessed their own long-lasting power source, there was no reason why he shouldn't walk. Even if he ran their power levels to zero, once the ship were underway he would be able to do without them completely anyhow.

He addressed the conveyance. "Cart. Go away. Please."

"Screw you," the cart dutifully replied.

As the cart scurried away in the direction of the *Guy*, he smiled broadly. *That simply does not get old!* He held the smile as he began trotting to the waiting *Guy* at a velocity his biological legs could never have attained. He quickly overtook the cart, and in his head, in time to the beat of his feet, he whistled a tune a century old. *From now on I'm taking some t-i-i-i-me for living,* he sang to himself as he jogged away, with the dismissed cart falling farther and farther behind, scurrying like an ignored puppy struggling to keep up.

About the Author

Ken Krawchuk is a life-long space enthusiast, an avid reader of science fiction, and an unabashedly unashamed Starship fanboy.

No Dogs on Mars is Ken's second major work of fiction. The first, *Atlas Snubbed*, is a pastiche parody sequel to Ayn Rand's *Atlas Shrugged*.

In his professional life, Ken is host of The Pennsylvania Project, a weekly talk radio show on WWDB in Philadelphia. In addition to a long career serving as an Information Technology geek, he also holds three United States patents related to database theory.

In his everyday life, Ken is a three-time Libertarian Party candidate for Governor of Pennsylvania, a Distinguished Toastmaster twice over, and a lover of IPAs, red Bordeaux, groaner puns, and alotta alliteration. This novel is his first opportunity to exercise his B.S. in Physics in quite some time.

He and his first wife Roberta have been married forever, or so it seems, and they have three adult daughters and four grandchildren (so far). In their copious free time, Ken and Bert always take some time for living, including whitewater canoeing, overnight backpacking, railroading, ocean cruising, and romantic candlelit dinners in front of a roaring fire, among many of the other finer things in life.

Lastly, Ken has already compiled detailed notes outlining a second Starship story, *No Dogs in Bed*. The apprentice domestic would approve.

Acknowledgements

I would be remiss if I didn't offer my heartfelt thanks to several fine people who helped make this book a reality. Let's start with my reviewers Cate and Rick Conti, Alex and Melanie Walsh, and David "Lord" Easlea. My youngest daughter Carissa Krupka not only reviewed it, but added quite a bit of humor. I also have to thank my patient editor Henry Whitney for all his Chicago Manual reminders and excellent plot suggestions. One person who definitely added a great deal to the book—yet never read it—is my marketing guru, Marc Bozzacco. Odds are that it's his fault you hold this book in your hands.

And lastly, let me repeat my words from the book's dedication and thank my dear wife Roberta for all her endless patience with my ramblings and poor puns as the book came together.

- Ken Krawchuk
November 14, 2020

About Martian Courts

This book was originally designed and written without any appendices, but the publisher insisted that the book be at least ninety-nine pages long. That left seventeen pages left to fill, so rather than expanding the font to a childish size, those extra pages could be employed in a more-meaningful manner; hence, this appendix.

That said, below are two chapters excerpted from a different novel by the author, *Atlas Snubbed*, which tell the story of the creation of the system of law used on Mars, and the rules of court which grew up around it. Granted, the locale for these chapters is a post-apocalyptic Las Vegas, but the justice system—and its fallout—remain the same for both planets. Enjoy!

CHAPTER 7 – DID YOU EVER HAVE TO MAKE UP YOUR MIND?

The gavel cracked.

"All rise!" the hastily recruited bailiff called out as the door to the judge's chambers opened.

"No!" Eddie cried automatically, stopping in the doorway. In front of him the courtroom was populated with dozens of people; half were already standing, half still sitting, with a few caught midway in the act of rising, uncertain whether to complete the action in either direction.

"Sit down, please!" he called out. "It's only me. You don't have to get up."

The standees sat as one as Eddie strode with a confidence he did not feel to take his seat behind the large, ornate desk upon the raised dais. He looked around the room uncertainly, wondering if he had somehow been transported through a magical mirror and was now looking back through it into the normal world he had left behind. He shook off the fantasy, steeled himself, and took a deep breath.

"All right, this court will come to order."

"Objection!" It was the bandit. He was manacled to a burly policeman, wrist-to-wrist, co-joined Siamese twins seated at a table midway between Eddie and the audience.

"What?" Eddie blinked myopically. The unexpected interruption had taken him by surprise. "What's your objection?"

The bandit fixed a squinting gaze upon Eddie and jabbed an accusing index finger in his direction. "You're no judge! Where's your robe? You have no power over me!"

"You're right," he admitted lightly. "I'm no judge, I have no robe, and I have no power over you. But I promise you I'll do my best to make sure you get a fair hearing."

"No! It's the law! This trial cannot proceed without a real judge!"

"Sure it can," Eddie explained patiently. "Because it's not the judge who's important here, it's the jury. You're accused of robbing that woman—" He pointed to the stunningly pretty young lady in the front row. "—at gunpoint, and it'll be the jury who'll decide your guilt or innocence, not me. I'm only here acting as sort of a referee. I'll be doing no judging today."

"But that's not what the law says a judge does!"

"It's what I do," he said simply.

"But if there's no judge, then you have to set me free!"

"Why's that?"

"Because you're no judge!"

"I'll be the judge of that. Better yet..." Eddie turned to the audience. "How many of you accept me as judge here today?"

Every hand in the audience went up. At the table in front of Eddie, the burly policeman raised his own manacled wrist, dragging along with it the wrist of the bandit, lifting both their arms into the air. A satisfied, mischievous smile spread across his husky face.

The bandit threw the man an annoyed scowl before jerking both their arms back down.

Eddie scanned the crowd. "Okay, it looks unanimous. Let's get going." He quickly estimated the number of people in the room and divided by seven. "Starting with you..." He pointed to a teenager at one end of the front row. "...begin counting off. Every seventh person, please take a seat in the jury box."

A panicked buzz of conversation instantly filled the air as the members of the audience reacted to the unexpected duty that was being asked of them.

"Objection!"

Patiently, Eddie faced the bandit. "What is it this time?"

"You can't do that! I know the law—I'm allowed to interview each prospective juror!"

"Interview them? What for?"

"I get to reject the ones I don't like!"

Eddie blinked twice. "You mean you want to stack the jury?"

The bandit hesitated; he hadn't thought of it in quite those terms before. "But it's my right!"

Recovering, Eddie flatly replied, "No it isn't. Picking and choosing jurors like that wouldn't be fair. We'll just take every seventh person, no questions asked." To the audience, he repeated, "All right, start counting. Every seventh person to the jury box, please."

"Objection!"

Sternly, Eddie shook a finger at him. "Listen: I said I'm not going to let you stack the jury!"

"But it's the law!"

"Whose law?"

Again, the bandit hesitated. This trial definitely wasn't following along the normal lines. He didn't know whose law it was; all he knew were the gopher holes of procedure. But he wasn't going to let ignorance stop him. "The laws of America!" he guessed with forced conviction.

Intrigued but not impeded, Eddie asked, "Which law of America? Explain it to me. I'm no lawyer."

Hesitation and exasperation simultaneously burst forth. "How the hell should I know?"

"Or I," Eddie concurred. He sat in thought for a moment, then added, as if talking to himself, "You know, I'm not sure the laws of America would apply in any case. It's been over a month since the X Project exploded, and we've heard absolutely nothing from the rest of the nation since then. There doesn't seem to *be* any America any longer." He paused again briefly. "And besides, I'm not certain theft is a federal crime anyhow." With a start he realized the root of his uncertainty: he had never before read the Constitution, nor had it been taught in the schools he attended. He dismissed the random thought and returned to the matter at hand. "Regardless, if you or I don't know the law, how could we possibly follow it? How else would you suggest that we choose a jury?"

Seeing his chance, the bandit interjected, "That's why you have to let me go! You're no judge, you have no law, and you have no jury. You have no power over me!"

Eddie waved an arm across the courtroom. "These people have accepted me as their judge. They will be your jury."

"But you have no law!" he repeated.

Eddie hesitated. He could not deny that the bandit had a valid point. Given the total evaporation of government in Las Vegas—not to mention Nevada and the former United States!—where could a basis be found for any law? But there *had* to be some touchstone he could use that would provide a firm foundation for conducting a court of law. *But what might that principle be?* he asked himself. Unbidden, in his mind's eye Eddie recalled the bright sunlight of a summer morning when he was ten years old. On that day, in a clearing of the woods, he had told the young Dagny what he planned to do when he grew up: to reach for the best within himself, to do whatever is right. *Whatever is right!* For him it had always been a self-evident goal, one that he had pursued all of his life; he could never understand why men would ever want to do otherwise. That commitment made by the child Eddie reached across the decades to come to his aid today in this moment of need. He nodded to himself. He knew what to do, and more importantly, he *knew* he knew. Shaking himself out of his reverie, he asserted, "The law is that you must do whatever is right."

The bandit scoffed. "Yeah, right. And what does *right* mean?"

"A fair question. Here's a fair answer: it's the Golden Rule. Do unto others as you would have them do unto you—and isn't that enough law for any man? It's all about having the right to live your own life, but also respecting the rights and property of others. "

"Bah!" the bandit cried with a flourish of his free hand. "Mere words! Bromides! High-sounding, meaningless words!"

"They're not mean—," he began, but the bandit cut him off.

"Then what rights do I—or does anyone else!—have? Tell me that!"

Eddie did not hesitate. "All right, let me spell it out for you: you have the inalienable right to live your life your way, without interference, pro—"

"Then let me out of here!" he interrupted again. "I was living my own life my own way when you guys interfered!" He shook his manacled arm in defiant demonstration of the truth of his statement.

Eddie ignored the outburst and continued as if it had not happened. "You have the right... *provided*—do you hear me?—*provided* that you respect the rights and property of others. You did not respect this woman's right to live her life her own way, even though she was respecting yours."

"Respect?" he sneered. "Don't talk to me about respect! Your entire capitalist system lacks respect! If a man has no money, your system would just let him starve! Doesn't a man's privation give him the right to take what he needs?" He gestured unconsciously toward the victim he had robbed.

Eddie shook his head. "Not if she has a right to her own life and property, too. You have a responsibility to respect that right, or else you can't expect others to respect yours." After a second, he added, "And I would think that men are compassionate enough that they wouldn't let another man starve."

The bandit ignored the aside, and replied with mocking sarcasm. "Exactly where did I pick up this 'responsibility' to her?"

Eddie ignored his contempt and answered sincerely. "Responsibility is an integral, inseparable part of your rights. Because for every right you enjoy, you have a corresponding responsibility to respect that right in others. So, for example, you have the right to live your life—but you have the corresponding responsibility to respect her right to live her own life. You have the right to your property—but you have the corresponding responsibility to respect the property of others. Rights and responsibility are two sides of the same coin."

"And what coin is that?"

"Liberty."

For several seconds after the echoes of his word died away, not a sound could be heard.

The bandit was first to react. "So you're saying that my rights come with strings attached?"

"Not strings so much as intertwined obligations. I'd call it personal freedom tempered by personal responsibility."

"And how far does this responsibility extend?" he inquired derisively. "What limit do you place upon my rights?"

Eddie considered the question for a moment. "To use an analogy, your right to swing your fist ends where her nose begins." At a sudden thought, he corrected himself. "No, wait; that's not quite correct. Even swinging your fist at someone shows a lack of respect. It stands to reason that threats of violence cannot be considered respectful, now can they?" He stared off into space for a moment, surprised at the truth of his own words.

The bandit hesitated as well, but for different reasons. Granted, he had come here today expecting to receive an education—but not one in philosophy! What did he care about philosophy? Still, he had to grudgingly admit that what Eddie was saying made sense on some fundamental level. Regardless, he could not let it stand; he had to extricate himself from this courtroom as a free man, and he could see that he was quickly running out of options. He had walked free every time he had been in court before; he had fully expected to do so again today—except that he found the solid legal granite he stood upon was quickly turning to philosophical sand. "But I have a right!" he repeated with hollow conviction, not knowing what else to say, as if the mere repetition would make it true, while understanding fully that it wouldn't.

"I agree," Eddie replied simply. "You have a right." He pointed to the victim. "And so does she. We all do. But like I said, we also have the responsibility to respect the rights of others, lest we throw away our own rights in the process. Abdicating that responsibility is what you're essentially accused of having done."

"And that's another thing!" he cried, attempting to pull the philosophical argument back into the realm of the legal. "No one's told me exactly what crime it is I'm being accused of committing!"

Momentarily at a loss, Eddie responded uncertainly. "I thought I did." Recovering, he pointed a finger at the victim. "Yes I did. You're accused of stealing money from that woman at gunpoint. I said that."

The bandit leaned forward across the table and his voice became suavely derisive. "Yes, But what *kind* of stealing are you talking about? Larceny, burglary, robbery, or what? First, second, or third, degree? Petit or grand? Misdemeanor or felony?"

Still wearing a perplexed expression, he replied, "Does it really matter?"

"Huh? Of course it does!"

"Why is that?"

Once again, the bandit was brought up short. "Uh..."

Eddie waited him out. When it became apparent no further words were forthcoming, he picked up the thread. "I'd venture to say that part of the problem with trials in the past was that the lawyers and judges relied too much on the words rather than on the deeds. Who really cares what it's called? Why over-classify? You're accused of taking that woman's property under threat of force, and that's all that matters. You did not respect her right to her life and property. Understand?"

Silence.

Seeing again that no answer was imminent, Eddie sat up straight in his chair, and to the audience, he politely requested, "Okay, now that that's settled, let's proceed. Every seventh person to the jury box, please."

"But I have a right!" the bandit repeated yet again even less convincingly than before, almost whining. No one troubled to reply, and he did not—*could* not—pursue the matter further; he had no idea in which direction he might take it. Unschooled though he was, he was more than intelligent enough to recognize the wisdom in the words of Eddie, and he could plainly see that the audience saw it, too. Stripped of any philosophical, legal, or dramatic defense, he decided it best to bide his time for the moment, and wait for other opportunities to present themselves. He subsided moodily.

Uncertainly the count-off began and gathered confidence as it progressed. In short order, four men and three women took their new seats in the jury box. The bandit grumbled inaudibly at the table in front of him, not looking up.

"Okay, let's have the victim tell her side of it. Miss?"

At his behest, the woman stepped up to the witness stand demurely and took a seat. All eyes were upon her, and not merely because she was a newly minted celebrity and a part of the show, but more so because she happened to be a stunningly beautiful woman. Only Eddie seemed to remain untouched and aloof. He nodded to her gravely. "All right, tell us what happened."

"Hey!" shouted the bandit. "Objection!"

"What now?" he asked patiently.

"She has to be sworn in!"

"Why is that?"

The bandit hesitated uncertainly. He was clearly not performing at his best this morning. "Uh... So that we know she's not lying?" He didn't sound too certain of his own assertion.

Eddie put a palm against his cheek, leaned on his elbow, and again looked perplexed. "But... But if she were going to lie, wouldn't she just lie about swearing to tell the truth? Either she's honest or she's not. It's up to the jury to take her at her word or not."

"Then what's to stop *me* from lying to *you*?"

"Nothing. Was there ever anything to stop you, except yourself?"

The bandit opened his mouth as if to say something, but no words came forth. His jaw closed and he wet his lips. The statement was true.

Eddie turned to the victim. "Proceed."

In an incongruently cheerful voice, she told her story of the evening in question exactly as it had happened, how she was walking home with the evening's receipts in her handbag, how the bandit had approached her and demanded the money at gunpoint, how she had complied and ran. In a minute, she was through.

"Do you have any questions for her?" Eddie asked the bandit.

"You bet I do!" The bandit stood and began to swagger around the table to approach the witness stand, but only made it as far as the length of the short chain on the manacles. Sporting a sardonic smile, the burly officer gently but insistently pulled him back to their table and into his chair; the bandit scowled at him menacingly but impotently. Regaining his poise somewhat, the bandit turned to the woman, addressing her from his seat.

"How did you catch me?"

She smiled prettily. "I didn't," she replied politely. "The police did."

"How did you know I was coming?" he pressed. "You guys were all ready for me!"

"The police did it," she replied, not the least bit put out for having to repeat herself. "They warned me you might try to rob me one night soon. And they were right!"

"How did *they* know?"

Smiling coyly, she replied, "You should probably ask them that."

"This is a waste of time," he grumbled. Turning to Eddie, he demanded, "I want to talk to the cops. Put the cops on the stand!"

"Have you any further questions for this woman?"

"No! Get the cops up there!"

Eddie dismissed the woman, and time stopped as she took her seat, every eye upon her. Again, only Eddie seemed above the delightful distraction.

Next he called up the policeman. With professional detachment, the man related how he had watched the entire incident from the third story bedroom of the busybody widow, how he had seen the masked bandit approach his victim, heard the demand for money, saw her throw her purse at him and run away, and how his men had stepped in and immediately apprehended the man. Finished with his tale, the policeman calmly sat there, hands folded in his lap, not offering any additional details.

Without waiting to be invited, the bandit demanded, "How come you were already there?"

"Me?" asked the policeman, a little too innocently. "You're asking me what I was doing in a woman's bedroom late at night?" He looked up to Eddie. "Do I have to answer that?"

Blushing, he replied. "No, of course not." To the bandit, he advised, "Let's stay on topic. Any other questions? Related to the trial, that is?"

The bandit felt trapped, an unusual circumstance for him. He was accustomed to being the man in command of every conceivable situation, yet he felt his grip on events loosening more and more with each passing second. "I... I...," he began, but could not finish. He nervously glanced right and left as if seeking escape. "I..." Something suddenly snapped within him and he brought both his fists down hard on the table in front of him, the resounding slam startling everyone. "How the hell did you know I was going to rob this woman?" he yelled. Someone at the back of the courtroom emitted a long whistle. Too late did the bandit realize his error—he had just admitted his guilt. Slack-jawed, he looked around him. The faces of the jurors were hard and closed. It was all over for him, he could tell.

Getting control of himself, he sat upright and folded his arms across his chest, his face blank, the manacles' chain pulled taut. They'd never tell him what he wanted to know, that was certain. There would be no education for him here today, no victory.

"Any other questions?"

The bandit did not reply. Arms folded, he stared straight ahead, eyes focused on nothing. The impression was that of a child pouting.

"Then we'll proceed."

Several other witnesses were called to testify, some of them police officers on the scene, others neighbors who had been watching from the safety of their own homes, each describing their viewpoint of the robbery.

Throughout it all, the bandit sat silent. For the first time in his nefarious career, he was at a complete loss; his mind raced, but it spun in circles; he simply could not think of any way out. There was no question he would be found guilty, irrespective of his blunt admission. He could not rely on esoteric errors of legal procedure, and he was certain he would not be able to bribe his way out; his only remaining chance was in fighting the sentencing.

The last witness completed his damning testimony, and Eddie addressed the bandit directly.

"Do you wish to call any witnesses?"

Sullen silence echoed across the room.

"I'll take that as a 'no.'" To the bailiff, he ordered, "Please take the jurors to the deliberation room so they can come to a verdict."

The bandit glimpsed another procedural avenue opening up to him, and without thinking, automatically took it. He sprang to life: "Objection!"

Again caught by surprise, Eddie could only reply, "What? What now?"

With a sinking feeling, the bandit realized that procedural objections fell upon deaf ears here; he may as well have remained silent. Nevertheless, the damage had been done, so he pressed on. "You're required to give them their instructions!"

"What instructions?" asked Eddie blankly.

The bandit snorted. "Lots of them! A big rigmarole about trying the facts and not the law. I've heard judges say it a thousand times!" He was interrupted by jeering laughter from the back of the room; the bandit ignored it.

Eddie was plainly confused. "Are you saying that I should try to influence the jury?"

Now it was the bandit's turn to be confused. "Huh?"

Patiently, Eddie explained. "They are the jury. They are the ones who must decide, and I'm not going to try to influence them in any way. As I said at the beginning, I'm a referee, not a participant. They listened to everything that was said, and now it's up to them to decide your guilt or innocence."

"Using your 'law?'" he sneered.

"That's up to them, too. I can't force my law or my opinions onto anyone. Nor should they listen to me, if I tried. That's what makes them the jury. They can judge both the law and the facts. If they believe it's all right for you to walk up to someone and demand money at gunpoint, then they'll acquit you. If not, they'll find you guilty. What is it I could possibly add to that? Or want to?"

"I..." He halted. Nothing further came out. Again, he was completely at sea. Deflated, he returned to his sullen pose.

After a respectful pause, Eddie turned to the bailiff. "Please take the jurors to the deliberation room." He gently clacked the gavel on the surface of his desk. "We'll recess until they decide."

As she left, one of the jurors called out over her shoulder, "You can bet it won't be long!"

The bandit sat up with a start, as if he were about to object to something, but thought better of it and subsided.

Standing up and stretching, Eddie commented, "In that case, I'll think we'll wait right here."

* * *

The jurors returned.

It could not have been more than three minutes; a bad sign for the bandit, to be sure. Their faces blank, the seven filed back into the jury box as the audience and Eddie reclaimed their own seats.

Once everyone had settled down, he asked, "Have you reached a verdict?"

One of the jurors stood up, the woman who had warned of a quick verdict. "Yes, Your Honor, we have."

Eddie could not help but wince at being addressed as "Your Honor," but tried not to let it show. "Well? What say you?"

"Guilty!"

The gallery sat silent. No one was surprised by either the verdict or the restrained reaction, but electric anticipation hung heavy in the air. They all knew what was coming next.

In the silence, Eddie locked eyes with the bandit. His words echoed clearly across the silent room. "You're one smart fellow, do you know that?" The bandit did not reply. "From what we've heard about how you planned out and executed your crime, and from what I saw of your defense, it's plain to me that you're more than a cut above your average crook." Still there was no reaction, so Eddie continued. "I spent a lot of time considering what sort of sentence might be appropriate if you were convicted, and until five minutes ago I still wasn't sure exactly what we should do. The idea of tossing you in jail is personally repugnant to me, not to mention the question of who pays the cost of keeping you there. Tell me: do you want to go to jail?"

The bandit remained silent at first, but then stirred in his seat. "No" was all he said.

Eddie nodded. "Then I think we can work out something that might be a little better for all of us." He sat up straight and assumed a more formal pose; the sentencing was about to begin. Many in the gallery straightened in unconscious imitation, sensing the moment of truth was at hand.

"Having been found guilty by a jury of your peers of not respecting the rights of another, I recommend the following sentence: by your actions you have demonstrated that you cannot be trusted to roam freely in our society, so I believe it appropriate that you be exiled from Las Vegas for the period of one year."

The audience murmured its surprise; it was not what they had expected to hear. The bandit did not react, and Eddie waited for silence before he continued.

"I further recommend that you spend your year confined to the vicinity of the Boulder Dam powerplant. While you are there, you will be presented with the opportunity to learn how the powerplant operates, and you shall be given the chance to apply your knowledge as a worker. If you choose to take the job, you will be paid a fair wage during your exile. But if you cause trouble, then the remainder of your year will be spent in jail here in town where you'll perform whatever menial labor is necessary to cover the cost of your board." He paused for a brief moment indicating he had finished, then added tentatively, "Okay?"

Caught off guard, the bandit gaped. "'Okay?' What do you mean, *okay*?"

"I mean, do you accept the sentence?" he explained succinctly, knowing full well he had no authority to impose it directly. As far as he was concerned, it was up to the bandit to accept it or not. He leaned slightly forward in his chair, attentively awaiting an answer. He fervently hoped the answer would be 'yes;' he wasn't entirely sure what he would do should the sentence be rejected.

The bandit did not react at first, but soon a small smile crossed his face. He had recognized the same absence of an alternative. "And what if I refuse?"

Eddie shrugged. "As I said, you're a smart fellow. I don't think you will."

The bandit sat for almost a full minute quietly considering his plight. Like Eddie, he was unsure of just what might happen, should he refuse. On the other hand, if he agreed, here was an opportunity to remove himself from the path of career criminal upon which he had long ago set himself. *Perhaps I should accept?* The bandit shrugged to himself. *And why not?* If it didn't work out, he could always return to a life of banditry. He silently reviewed his options one last time, and as the last of the minute began to die, he finally spoke: "I accept exile." He smiled to himself, thinking, *Once again I get off without a jail term! My record is intact!*

The audience burst into spontaneous applause. Rather than the somber moment which characterized most sentencing, the mood was one of unexpected jubilation. Many of the men had feared that a milquetoast Eddie might prove to be too lenient, while others feared the inexperienced judge would overreact with an unduly heavy-handed response; but having the bandit not only removed from the company of the law-abiding citizenry for a reasonable period and also set on a path to rehabilitation allayed all such doubts. Not only had vengeance been served this day, but justice as well.

Two members of the audience, obviously friends of the accused, rushed forward and shook the bandit's hand enthusiastically, slapping him on the back and laughing. The attractive woman who was the victim rested her two adoring eyes squarely upon Eddie, obviously pleased with the result. The jurors were shaking hands with one another, but each of them kept catching Eddie's eye as well, giving him a brief nod of appreciation. The policeman sat alone to one side, and when his eyes met Eddie's, he flashed him an energetic, two-fisted "thumbs up." Similar reactions came from every corner of the room. As with the defeat of the raiders, Eddie found himself once again cast in the role of the hero.

His work here done, Eddie rose to leave. To his surprise, as he did, all conversation came to a quick, abrupt halt. All eyes were upon him now; he felt self-consciously aware of their stares as he stood alone on the dais before them. He felt it incumbent upon himself to say something profound, but he retreated instead into the trite. To the bandit, he said simply,

"Welcome aboard." Looking to the audience, he added, "This court is adjourned."

The crowd exploded into cheers as Eddie turned and left.

CHAPTER 9 – CRAWL BACK UNDER MY STONE

The crook cowered.

The unfortunate man had little choice but to hide himself. The day had been pure hell for him, a damnation that had started early and continued to accelerate with each passing hour. Hence, he hid; he *had* to hide!

As with most damnations, his had sprouted from a combination of great pride and righteous determination. Standing in front of the Las Vegas jury that had just convicted him of theft, he flatly rejected the sentence of three months' exile they had decreed as his punishment. "I do not recognize this court's right to try me!" he had cried defiantly. If they needed his sanction to make the proceedings legal, he was not going to give it. "Go ahead and plaster my face around town on your 'exiled' posters; I will not help you pretend that you are administering justice!" he asserted brazenly. "I will have no part of it!" His brave words earned him the admiration of his criminal peers; and when he stalked out of the courtroom unmolested, they slapped him on the back and pumped his hand energetically. By now, everyone in town had heard how you need not accept the sentence of the jury, but in the months since the new brand of trials had begun, none had chosen to stand against their verdict—until today. The crook was riding high on top of his thieves' world as a man in sole control of his fate. Standing in the mid-morning sun in front of the courthouse, he snapped his fingers at the building in criminal contempt, to a backdrop of his contemporaries' raucous applause. *He* sure showed *them!*

But the initial glow of triumph did not last long. The first crack in his newfound renown arrived only a few hours later, innocently enough, on the wings of humor during lunch at the honky-tonk near the Transcontinental station. As he sat with his co-workers and related the proud tale of the morning's trial over a fat mug of foamy, yellow ale, on a whim one of his companions took on a mischievous grin and reached out to snatch the mug from in front of the unsuspecting crook.

"Hey!" the crook cried. "That was *my* beer!"

His friend laughed into the pilfered beer as he sipped it, spraying white foam across the tabletop. "You're right! It *was* your beer!" With that, he downed the drink in a single, gulping swig.

"Why, you—," the crook began, but his companions only laughed.

"Go tell it to the jury!" the friend jabbed as he wiped off his chin. "If they'll even bother to listen to you!"

The others at the table laughed in unison at the joke being played on the unfortunate crook; they knew for a fact the man could never call on the jury to defend his rights ever again. So the victimized crook found himself reluctantly joining in the laughter; and for the first time that day, he found he had little other choice.

"Just having a little fun," asserted his friend. "Hey, let me buy you another." He signaled to the lovely barmaid, and she brought the crook a fresh mug. But no sooner than the beverage hit the table when another man snatched it up before the thirsty crook could even begin to reach for it.

"Hey!" he cried again.

"Tell it to the jury!" the man echoed. Sipping noisily, in a single, fluid motion he rose and spun away from the table to escape with his booty.

The results were similar with the third, fourth, and fifth beers the hapless crook attempted to order. The joke had rapidly worn thin, and the crook was forced to retreat in anger from the table to take a seat at the bar. Moodily he claimed an empty stool and ordered yet another beer. The beverage arrived swiftly, and he slid a large silver coin across the surface of the bar in payment; the proprietor smiled, pocketed the gleaming disc, and walked away.

"Hey!" the crook called to the retreating man. "Where's my change, buddy? That was a willie, you know!"

"What change?" the proprietor inquired innocently, brazenly holding his gaze.

The tableau held for several seconds before the crook realized he was being had yet again, and worse yet, that he was again left without recourse. Stymied, he angrily dashed the contents of the mug into the proprietor's face and stormed away, heading for the door. But in his anger he did not notice the foot that unexpectedly shot out in front of his, and with a squawk he tumbled over it to fall hard onto the wooden floor. The patrons laughed, and several heckled the unfortunate crook as he clambered to his feet and continued his interrupted retreat, red-faced with impotent anger. He slammed the swinging doors wide and fled the scene, once again being left with no other choice.

The end of the afternoon found him progressing further down the road to damnation: when his employer paid him his day's wage, it was only half the amount that was due him.

"Where's the rest of my money?" he demanded.

"You spent the whole morning in court. You're lucky you're getting that much!"

"But the trial lasted less than an hour, and I was on the job before ten!" he protested. "I deserve more than a half day's pay!"

"Go cry to the jury," suggested the cheating employer. "If they'll listen, that is!" He knew they wouldn't; not now. The news of the mischievous escapade at lunch had spread quickly.

The short-changed crook had no choice but to head for home; and when he arrived, he discovered his troubles had ratcheted to a new level, for while he was away someone had kicked in his door and ransacked the house; a quick glance revealed that most everything of value was missing. Granted, he did not live in the best of neighborhoods, and his friends were all of the same moral caliber as he, but there used to be some modicum of honor among thieves. Yet in light of his refusal to accept the sentence of the jury, that negligible amount of honor had vanished in a flash.

Open-mouthed he stared at the devastation a moment longer before blind anger washed over him. "Damn them all to Hell!" he frothed, hurling his hat to the messy floor in exasperated rage, his curse spanning not only his so-called friends, but also the members of the morning's jury. Ignoring the mess, he stepped hatless out onto the street, leaving the breached door open behind him. There was no point in closing it now. *What next?* he snapped angrily at the unknown judges of his unwitnessed mood.

BLAM! The dust puffed at his feet where the bullet had hit. "Run, you lousy bastard!" a disembodied voice yelled. *BLAM!* the revolver reported again, this time shattering the door jamb alongside his head, scattering splinters painfully across his cheek.

The panicked crook immediately took the advice to heart. Crouching low, he scurried around the corner of his home anxiously awaiting a third bullet, which fortunately never came. Discharging firearms within the city limits of Las Vegas was itself a crime, regardless of the intended target, but such niceties apparently meant nothing to his unseen attacker.

"You stay away from my girl!" demanded the anonymous assailant of the fleeing crook. "Or else! Because it's open season on the likes of you, you damned Exile, you! Get out of town! *Now!* And *stay* out!"

The poor crook's mind was in a whirl as he fled; he had no idea which girl his invisible nemesis might have meant—or if any girl existed at all! But girl or no girl, the heart of his message was crystal clear.

Sunset found him cowering in the back room of an abandoned store on the seediest side of town. In mere hours, his status had devolved from that of a free citizen to apprehended suspect to convicted criminal to hunted animal, leaving him with all the rights of an animal, specifically: none. He was an outlaw—literally a man outside the law—and as such, no longer entitled to call upon the court for protection. Nor was there any viable alternative; even the former crime bosses in town obeyed the new rules. There was more profit in it.

"Damn!" he cursed under his breath, cautiously quiet lest he inadvertently give his presence away. *What do I do now?* he demanded of himself, yet full well knowing the answer.

With a sigh he came to the only decision possible: later on, in the very wee hours of the morning—which was the *only* time the streets of Las Vegas ever emptied out!—he would slink back to the police station, turn himself in, repent, and accept the sentence of the court. One final time, he found himself with no other choice. Yes, he'd have to move to Boulder City or take a job as a farmhand at one of the outlying ranches, but the three months of his exile would pass quickly—or so he hoped. And even if it didn't, his existence would surely improve over what had promptly become one of the worst days of his life.

Read the entire story via AtlasSnubbed.com.

And that makes it ninety-nine pages. Print it!